FOUR
PART
HARMONY

by the same author

Family Myths and Legends
Indefinite Nights
Write to Me

FOUR PART HARMONY

Patricia Ferguson

André Deutsch

First published in Great Britain in 1995 by
André Deutsch Limited
106 Great Russell Street
London WC1B 3LJ

CIP data for this title is available
from the British Library.

ISBN 0 233 989161

Printed in Great Britain by
WBC, Bridgend

1

ON THE STEPS OF THE HALL JANET STOPPED altogether, and thought about just turning round and walking straight back home again. The picture was so tempting that she automatically turned to face the pavement, but then she hit on imagining what the end of that homeward flight would really be like, the smell of cat-pee in the hallway, the cold stairwell, her own tidy but particularly empty flat all lying in wait for her and an entire evening still to get through.

And they'd never have me again, not if I just don't turn up. Or could I say I'd had an accident, felt ill?

I'd still have it hanging over me, then.

Janet saw herself standing in her chilly front room, a person who had pointlessly chickened out. No. It was no good. She would have to go through with it.

She turned and climbed heavily up the steps. Fear encumbered her whole body.

Why have I done this? I must've been mad, she told herself. Bitterly she yanked at the great door, which rattled but refused to move until she had seen its little notice, which read PUSH. Janet shoved, teeth clenched. Inside neon strips hummed. The corridor walls fluttered with posters. The door groaned to behind her.

1

There was no one about.

'Yeah?'

Janet jumped. Behind her, in a sort of panelled kiosk in the wall, stood a small fat man in a peaked hat like a bus conductor's. He brought his hand up from beneath the counter. There was a tiny roll-up wedged between the fingers like a dirty little ring.

'I help?'

'Um . . . I've come for an audition.'

The man looked no less blank.

'With the choir.'

'Uh. Straight on.' He was already turning round. 'And turn left.' A plastic chair hissed gently beneath his weight.

'Oh, er, thanks,' said Janet to the back of his head. She set off, trying not to make too much noise with her heels, past a long series of doors, all painted pale green with little plaques on them to hold names. But all the plaques were empty. At the end she followed the corner round to two large glass doors, and, seeing nothing else to do, opened one of them and slid through.

Slower now, on tiptoe, she made her way along another huge corridor, this time opening every few yards onto rooms full of enormous horrible things, straining metal boiler-like objects with stumpy metal feet and tentacles of concertina'd piping, emitting throbbing and hissing noises and once actual flames. Right at the end was a great closed door with the warning radioactive black and yellow insignia on it, and NO UNAUTHORISED ENTRY.

Bloody funny place to sing, thought Janet, and giggled nervously as she reached the far corner, turned left, and came at last upon a rather faded cardboard sign, reading **CHORALE SOCIETY** in handwritten copperplate, with an arrow pointing up at the stone staircase.

At the top of the stairs and round the corner a neat elderly man was sitting at a table. He had a clean brown face, glasses, a bit of white hair. He smiled when he saw Janet, and rose, introduced himself, and held out his hand.

Janet gave it a little shake, hardly able to speak for nerves. Already she wished she had been listening when he'd said his name. He gave her a form to fill in, and a biro, and hung about whistling softly through his teeth while she filled it in; name, address, date of birth, voice. Voice?

What? What were you supposed to put there? Janet thought, rather panicky: small, but not bad? In tune? Can't get very high?

Alto, she wrote, then looked up sharply. Was that the right word? Wasn't it short for contralto? Or would that be affected?

Sod it, thought Janet, it's only a choir, it's not a job, it's not important. As she thought this her heart began to knock so hard she could feel it beating in her throat.

Sight-reading, I've never done any sight-reading . . .

She had found her old hymn-book and tried practising but without a piano to tell her whether she was right or not she had no idea how well or how badly she could do, even without some bored or embarrassed or sniggering expert listening in and judging her.

And it's all Pass or Fail, thought Janet, trying to breathe slowly. If you weren't good enough you were out. No democracy at work here. No sparing of feelings. No messing about calling it musically challenged.

Janet snorted a little, and cleared her throat.

'Ah, is there anywhere I can get a drink of water, please?'

The old chap with glasses looked up. He had a dark brown suit on.

'Of course, of course,' he said. He was affable, thought Janet, getting up helplessly. He opened a door, disappeared, and came back almost immediately with a paper cupful. 'Here you go. Bit warm I'm afraid.' Behind him as the door swung to Janet glimpsed another tangle of pipes and rows of Bunsen burners.

'Thanks. What is this place?'

'It's the university physics building.'

'Oh.' Jesus, thought Janet, and hordes of wild-eyed men

in spectacles and white coats hurtled down the corridors past the rooms full of bulging radioactive tanks and boilers while sirens wailed *Garooga Garooga* and gases liquefied and glass shattered before the final almighty explosion KABOOM—

'Is it here every week then?'

'Oh yes. Very nice lecture hall, you see. Acoustics very good.'

'Oh.'

'So . . . you're from Bonnie Scotland, then.'

'How did you guess?' Janet smiled back, on automatic. A door banged somewhere, and she jumped as footsteps sounded.

'Here we are,' said the old chap, as the footsteps came rather slowly up the stairs. 'Evening, Robert.'

'Stanley.'

'This is, ah, Miss McIver.'

'Good, good.' Absent, unbuttoning his coat. Younger than she. Glasses, and thinning already at the front. 'Will you come in please?' Pushing at another big door.

The hall was full of enclosed space; an auditorium. A great wooden platform ran along the floor, dotted with Bunsen burners and small square sinks, and the wall behind it was all immense roller-blackboard, with bits of chalked scribble here and there, sums like whole paragraphs, brackets, arrows.

'Right, right, right. Have you prepared anything?' Opening the piano, was it there all the time, or did they wheel it in and out?

'Ah, I haven't any music, I thought I'd, you know, sing unaccompanied, if that's okay – '

'Yes, yes. Stand there, right. Yes. Go ahead please.'

Jane stood still. She thought of the right note, testing it in her head, skimming through to the last line, which she would miss altogether if she started too high. Right then. She drew breath.

4

'Oh where, tell me where, is your Highland laddie gone?
Oh where, tell me, where, is your Highland laddie gone?
He's gone with streaming banner, where noble deeds are done,
And, oh, in my heart, I wish my laddie home.'

More? She met his eyes. 'Yes, okay, lift your head a little, will you? Sing to the back of the hall.'

Louder, thought Janet, beginning the second verse. Nerves gave her pretty, unremarkable voice a gentle light vibrato, and the sound filled her with pleasure. She raised her head, and sang, she knew as well as she could. When she had finished the second verse she gave him a little questioning look, and he said, 'Yes, thank you very much', so that was right, glad I didn't do the last one, don't want him getting bored—

A girl's voice, she thought as she neared the piano. No change there, no matter what's happened to the rest of me. No change yet.

'Erm, sight-reading . . . here, take this. Don't bother too much about the words. I mean, pronunciation,' he added vaguely. He sat down at the piano, played a chord, and looked at her, his glasses flashing in the neon.

Janet looked at the music in horror, then at him. Not even a few minutes to look through it, hum over a tricky bit? And Jesus it wasn't even in English, it was in— She opened her mouth to say, Look, I've never done this before, hang on a minute, but he bounced straight into the introduction, hell, hell, seethed Janet, her eyes dashing about, where was he, he was there, there, right, G sharp, four four, Oh God is it me, yes—

She quavered into song. He played away steadily, not looking up, as if he was on his own, which he was most of the time. Lost, lost, no there, and—

'Yes,' he said at the end. She'd just about finished when he did, sung out loudly on the last note, feeling foolish, having missed out the entire phrase before it.

'Have you done much sight-reading?'

'Never before,' said Janet instantly, gratefully. 'I—'

'It does', said the man, 'tend to come a bit with practice.'

Emphasised the bit, Janet thought. She felt desperate.

'Sing this, will you?' He played some twiddle. Janet sang it.

'And this.' Scales.

'Not much range,' he said, after a minute or so.

'No.' said Janet apologetically. Oh please, please.

'Still.' He stood up, unsmiling. 'Second alto, I think. Where's your form? Here.'

He scribbled, handed it over.

'Second alto?'

'Yes. Ah, give it to Mr Laidlaw, will you, outside?'

Oh. Oh, I'm in, thought Janet, and a great wave of triumphant joy lifted her, all the lovelier for being held in, not clapped at or laughed over but clutched tight together along with her precious form for Mr Whatwasit—

'Rehearsal's in five minutes,' said the man. He opened a little hard suitcase and flipped through some papers inside it.

Janet went out to find the affable old chap, Mr Thing. She was trembling with happiness. Outside a vast number of people, variously scented, bearded, chatting, had crammed themselves up to the door. Among them the old chap looked rather small. She squeezed her way through to him. 'Erm, I'm to give you this—'

'Ah. Good news.' He beamed down at her. 'Well done,' he said, warm, light, a gentle baritone, oh, I can sing, thought Janet. *I can sing.* If I can't do anything else, I can sing.

2

PETER WAS LATE, SO ANNIE HAD A GOOD HALF HOUR to discuss him.

'We're on the verge,' she said to Joe, starting off. She pushed her long dark hair back from her forehead. Joe saw her and Peter lying side by side on a real verge on a motorway, holding hands, faces turned skywards; she'd said just the same thing last time. He picked up his pint, and drank deeply.

'We had this terrible row. I talked him into going for a walk. And he was just, you know, determined not to enjoy it. We saw a fox, and he wasn't interested, I got so fed up—'

Annie stopped suddenly. It had been so unkind of Peter, refusing to be pleased by the fox. She saw her own delight, her little leap, and pointing,

'Oh Peter, look!'

Just a few yards away the fox had been lying in the sun, stretched out on its side on what turned out to be a big piece of flattened cardboard.

'Like a dog on a hearthrug!'

Hearing her it had risen without haste, stretched its back legs, given her and Peter a brief indifferent once-over and made off into the bushes.

7

'Oh Peter!' She had turned to him, smiling; and seen his face.

And then just laid right into him, not only saying lots of things best left unsaid but saying them in wild bursts, despite all that lying awake night after night putting her most justified complaints and requests into proper order, so that when the time came a reasoned measured once-and-for-all precision-bombing would just about pound him flat. As it was the whole lot had gone off at once with nothing to show for it; even at the time she'd felt herself to be jabbering.

'Didn't know you were such a nag,' he'd said distantly, when she'd finally come to a stop.

Disaster. And she was filled now with anxious doubt, not only about the complaints and requests, which had sounded so perplexingly dim and vague when uttered, but about the snub that had so provoked her in the first place. Was it really cruel, just refusing to share a pleasure? Hadn't she really been angry with him all along, for needing so much prodding to come out with her on such a fresh sunny day, and then not bothering to pretend to enjoy himself? Could it be right, after all, to be angry with someone just for being honest?

'We had this terrible row,' she said again. 'About everything. Actually I—' Annie stopped abruptly. I told him he ought to chuck the thesis, she had been about to say, but found suddenly that she did not want to see Joe's reaction to this after all.

In fact the thesis had figured only slightly in the projected list of complaints and requests, and Annie had given a great deal of thought to ways of mentioning it without in any way seeming to dismiss or belittle it. When she had first started seeing Peter she had quickly come to look on the thesis as a sort of unusually powerful rival, one perfectly ready to wait about neglected for a while until Peter should eventually return to it, more long-suffering wife than alternative girlfriend. Her only real recourse had been a resolute, active non-jealousy. Previous girlfriends, Annie gathered, had simply made too many demands on his time and attention; they had selfishly or neurotically refused to give him the space and tranquillity he needed to concentrate. He needed whole weekends, he needed weeks at a time; if that was what it took, Annie thought, she would make sure that he had it, and when at last it was all done and finished they would both know why and how . . .

Annie's thoughts had always rather trailed off at this point, for the notion of being in effect owed grateful love was not exactly attractive, hinted in fact at not being loved for yourself alone; and more than once the trailing thoughts had gathered themselves together into the very much bleaker No One Loves Me At All.

'Why can't he just finish the bloody thing?' she had finally asked Joe furiously one evening, and it had felt like pure defeat, to admit thus to boredom, frustration, and jealousy. Hadn't all the other girlfriends admitted to them too, on their way to becoming ex-girlfriends?

'I've stopped seeing it as a wife,' she'd said. 'It's really more of a sick relation. Bed-ridden. Constant attention, you know, like Bunbury.'

'Sorry?'

'In *The Importance of Being Earnest*, d'you remember? It's really just an excuse to get you out of anything you don't want to do.'

Joe hadn't met her eyes at that one. Noting another milestone, Annie had thought, watching him, on the way to ex-girlfriendhood: not taking the thesis quite seriously anymore.

'Not so much sick as moribund actually. On a sodding life-support machine.'

'I think it's real as well,' said Joe cautiously, after a pause.

Annie had sighed, for she knew that this was true. It was *real* all right, there were piles and piles of it really to trip over on the way to the bathroom in the middle of the night, and stacked in the hall, in boxes in the front room, in files even in the kitchen on a high shelf above the pots and pans. All that careful tiny handwriting, with arrows and additions in different coloured inks, all those various editions and early drafts typed up on different machines by different hands over how many years now, ten? eleven? Piles of hours in every room, piles of days, weeks, months, and years.

'It's ruining his life.'

'It's not that bad.'

'It is, it is, he can't take anything else seriously, he can't enjoy anything, he can't commit himself—'

To me, was the obvious ending to that one. Annie had scowled, knocked back her white wine spritzer. It was hard work, keeping discussions of the thesis on the right concern-for-Peter level. Getting down to concern-for-self, she felt dimly, must be just another turning on poor old Joe's ex-girlfriends' guide.

'You must have heard all this before,' she had said rather coldly. But Joe had only smiled.

But I never meant to tell him to chuck it, she thought now. I didn't mean it. It just came out, because I was so upset about the fox. Wish I'd never seen it, wish it had done its snoozing somewhere else. He'd sounded all right over the telephone though, hadn't he? Just as if nothing had happened. In a hurry to ring off, perhaps, but that was normal too.

'Lots of people give up,' she said aloud. 'They realise, you know, that it's just not them.'

Joe, who had been day-dreaming on his own account, took a second or two to catch up.

'Oh, you mean – Peter's never felt like that, though. You know he hasn't.'

He ought to then. He should, thought Annie, and the vivid strength of her longing, which was that Peter be as he was but different, made her hope once more that words, if she could only find the right ones, could achieve this tricky double.

10

'Wish I could burn it,' she said, after a pause.

Joe smiled. 'Hester had a go.'

'What, the solicitor?'

'Yes. Made off with Chapter Two, put it in the office shredder, sent it back in a Jiffy bag without so much as a farewell note attached.'

They laughed: Annie pretending not to have heard the story before, and in just those words, from Peter himself; Joe pretending not to mind telling Peter-stories, though doing so in fact depressed him, turned him, he felt, into just that fellow Peter-acolyte Annie seemed to expect him to be. The eunuch in the harem, he thought, rather surprising himself. No, that was going much too far, what had brought that on?

All this talk of him, I suppose. Her talking like this not because I'm her friend but because I'm his, an expert with twenty years of Petering to look back on. I'm jealous, I suppose. Still. A bit.

At the pub door Peter saw them laughing together but was instantly diverted by another sighting of the polar-bear man, a regular whose overcoat, an exotic whitish thing of swaggering romantic cut, was topped by an immense, slightly grubby white fur collar, which lay heavily across his shoulders like a big woolly arm; as he leant against the crowded bar it was easy to imagine the great, friendly bear squeezed in beside him, to construct their cosy affectionate home life together while Annie wiped her eyes; I can still make her laugh, anyway, thought Peter, glancing over towards her again. No, not laughing now. Just sitting there, the two of them, neutral, obviously waiting. So that was all right, he came nowhere near thinking. He put up one hand and pushed back his hair. It was pretty hair, still fair, with a graceful childish wave. He was not aware of how often he touched it. Again he ran his fingers through it, as if nervously: was Annie in one of her moods? and moved in.

11

3

STANLEY WAS MAKING PUFF PASTRY, AND HAD JUST reached the stage he liked best, dabbing on the neat little squares of butter, folding the pastry over them, and gently, ruthlessly, squashing the whole thing flat.

From the living room the television muttered and applauded, taking the edge off the quiet. Stanley wasn't trying to listen. He sliced more butter into squares, and addressed the committee: You know how I feel, thought Stanley. He picked up his rolling pin again.

They were all in their usual seats in the White Hart after rehearsal, all of them for once, even dopey Albert.

I know he's good, Stanley went on. He made the committee nod and murmur in agreement. I know he's good. I'm not denying it. I may not hit it off with him myself, dare say that's my fault just as much as his, sort of thing; but the fact is, we just can't afford him.

More flour. Turn.

And they would all agree, glad they couldn't afford him, chilly miserable bugger that he was, with never a word of praise for anyone, always sighing and closing his eyes in pain, all theatrical, and sneering outright at the tenors and charging off home like a shot afterwards, too high and mighty for a quick one. And Mrs Walton had cried; she had come to Stanley in actual tears.

12

Butter.

In tears! he reminded the committee. Twenty-three years she'd been with us. Hardly missed a rehearsal. Sang her heart out every concert. And sold more than two dozen tickets every time. I mean quite apart from everything else that's two dozen tickets we'll never sell again.

'There are ways and means,' said Stanley aloud in his kitchen. Carefully he turned the pastry through ninety degrees, and let old Geoff have a go:

There are ways and means, old Geoff would say, if you want to raise the quality of a choir. We did it at St Albans. New conductor, knew what he wanted, lots of dead wood. He didn't say, 'Right, auditions all round', he didn't chuck out thirty per cent. He took his time. He made it clear what he wanted. What standard. Wouldn't, you know, wait about for stragglers. And people realised, they left off their own bat – I haven't got time anymore, I've taken up woodwork, that sort of thing. You know. Saved face. And it only took a term. That's how we did it at St Albans. But this one. He wouldn't wait.

'Because he couldn't care less,' said Stanley, squeezing the pastry into the plastic bag he had ready and setting it in the fridge to cool for a while. He washed his hands and went into the living room still wearing his blue striped apron, turned the television set up and sat down. The room was very tidy and clean. Stanley had come late to housework. Often, as he polished or dusted, he thought remarks at his wife.

'You see? Nothing to it, is there? Don't know what all the fuss was about.'

He leant his head back now against the pale green dralon. No time for television, he thought at Amy, but all the same he sat there for several minutes while a lot of little bats flew in and out of a cave somewhere, and gave birth while hanging from the ceiling by their feet. Now and then, it seemed, they missed the catch as the babies popped out, whereupon a writhing carpet of glossy cave beetles far below flowed over one another to devour the helpless newborn bats alive.

'Disgusting,' said Stanley, without heat.

The bats had pleasant enough little doggy faces, and bodies that started off well – normal furry shoulders and so on – but just after their waists or thereabouts they trailed off suddenly into a disconcerting vague flimsiness, and a very sketchy half-hearted attempt at proper bottoms. And when they were on the ground they could only haul themselves about on their forearms as if on crutches, integral skin-covered crutches of elongated bone.

Something stirred in Stanley's mind, something to the pattern of, I don't know why you watch this stuff.

'It's often so lovely, the colours and everything.'

Stanley did not exactly think Amy's reply for her. There was a short gap instead, an Amy's-reply-shaped hole in his awareness, after which he rose and switched channels, putting the crippled bats out of mind with a few minutes of ordinary car-chasing and yells.

Bloody rubbish, thought Stanley more comfortably. He turned the sound down so that he would just be able to hear it from the kitchen, so I'll know when the news comes on, he thought, and went back to his pastry.

Chilled nicely. He took the bowl of cooked steak-and-kidney out too, and inspected its cold jellied succulence. It was going to be another perfect pie. He floured his rolling pin and his own large clean fingers.

Oh yes and him. That Robert. He was out. His days were numbered, his time was up.

'Singing in Latin,' said Stanley scornfully to the pastry. He stood for a moment looking down at it. From this angle it had a huddled look, as if it were hunching its shoulders in lumpy resignation or despair.

'Now then,' said Stanley kindly. He touched it lightly, took up his rolling pin, and with sudden vigour and energy flattened it almost at a stroke.

14

4

VICKI WAS OUT WHEN HE GOT HOME. RUSSELL, without taking his coat off, made the bed, put some washing on, and washed up the breakfast things, for it was his turn that week. When everything was finished he noticed the state the kitchen floor was in, and mopped it carefully with some stuff held to dry to a perfect shine. After that he had no option but to open the damn telephone bill, which while bad enough was not, it turned out, quite as bad as he had feared. Paying it would empty his account, all but three pounds. If he stayed in all week and took sandwiches to work he would make it, just about.

Meanwhile, supper: small can baked beans, 15p; whole-meal toast, well, 2p at the most; scrape of Flora didn't count; two raw carrots, what, 2p again? but good for you, and a cup of tea; the whole thing no more than 25p, which sounded very little until you translated it into old money, when five shillings had been a whole week's pocket money. Russell often put prices into old money, generally to stop himself buying something he ought to do without, new tapes, cans of lager, cigarettes before a party.

'Seventeen-and-six for a biro!' he would exclaim at Vicki. 'Milk six bob a pint!' And he could remember it costing one-and-tuppence.

'Whole afternoon in the swimming pool, two-and-six, cross the road to the chippy, get six penn'orth of chips!' he had reminisced to Vicki only the week before and been very taken aback by the unmistakable youth-boredom face she had made in reply. He had assumed that the speed with which such memories had become comically antique was a joke they could share. But the five years' difference in their ages meant that she couldn't remember old money at all. And it had become clear to him lately that she had no real interest in the past, his own or in general – anyone over thirty was in the same vague job-lot as far as she was concerned.

She'd just been pretending, then, when they'd first begun. Obviously. He remembered taking her for a walk round the City, not St Paul's, though that was of course the best building of all time anywhere, but to the little churches scattered about it, pointing out to her the gouges left by shrapnel in the walls of St Mary-le-Strand, and the stone before the front door there, worn to a trough by so many feet, and the buckled flags in the little courtyard, a Hogarth print come alive and flanked by roaring buses.

'Dickens's parents got married here!'

And to St Bride's, that miracle of rebuilding. 'They should have done all London up like this!' He had pointed out the new keystones, not angels anymore but local post-war dignitaries, one of them clearly bespectacled, and she had laughed out loud. Amused for the moment, he thought now.

He got up, sighing, and began to prepare his five-bob supper, and in the middle of scraping the second carrot the thought of the tribunal suddenly swung up and hit him so hard that he had to stop for a moment and hold onto the edge of the work-surface. Funny, he thought, how it kept coming at him out of the blue like that, several times a day at the moment and first thing every morning.

The telephone rang, and it was Barney.

'How you doing?'

16

'Not so bad.'

'All set? You know, for next week?'

Telepathy, thought Russell, without pleasure. 'I was just thinking about it actually.'

'It'll be a walkover, I just talked to Julia. Thought I'd let you know. She says she won't be there, she's not sure she saw anything.'

'What? Are you sure?'

'Yup. You're in the clear, mate. Thought I'd just let you know.'

'Oh, that's great, oh, thanks—'

'Don't thank me, I didn't lean on her or anything. She just came out with it. "I came in too late," she says.'

'Too late? There was nothing to see, he took a swing at me, I'd just caught hold of him, that's all—'

'Look, I believe you. Anyway. It's the moonlighting they'll be most pissed off about.'

'But you—' said it'd be a walkover, thought Russell hotly, you just can't bear to see me out of the shit, can you?

There was a pause.

'Still it was only the once, wasn't it,' said Barney. 'As far as they're concerned.'

'Yeah,' said Russell. There was another silence.

'So,' said Barney eventually, clearly giving up, 'you're on velvet, nothing to worry about. Just be calm and polite and don't act guilty.'

'I wasn't going to.'

'Fancy a drink later?'

'Can't. Skint.'

'My treat then. Come on, do yourself a favour.'

'All right. Nine-ish?'

'Great. See you.'

Russell, ringing off, put the potato peeler down and went into the bedroom. He owned three suits. He took them out one by one. The pinstripe his mother had bought him when he was seventeen, he'd worn it with a salmon-pink kerchief, must've looked a right prat, and he could still get

17

the trousers on but wouldn't be able to sit down; some old boy's best, passed on by his mum when the old boy died, well-cut tweeds right back in fashion now but completely weekend-in-the-countryfied, it'd look like fancy dress to any ordinary official mind; and an Oxfam with padded shoulders, in which he had more than once leant against doorways flicking a coin: they were all hopeless, they were all instant dismissal, anyone would think he was taking the piss. Ordinary clothes, then, why not? After all, the whole business was a farce, everyone did extra shifts when they had to, everyone had to defend themselves now and then. He was being made an example of, he thought, set up, to keep everyone else on their toes: it wasn't fair. I mean it's not that I'm so innocent, he told himself, going back to the beans, but I'm not that guilty either. A bit of a maverick, that's me. I go my own way. You've got to bend the rules sometimes. You've got to survive.

It was pleasant to apply such phrases to himself; and exciting. He thought of Vicki still bouncing up and down at her Dancercise, silly girl, all that aerobics and then lighting up with her mates in the pub afterwards. She was all right, Vicki, he thought, suddenly sentimental.

And good old Julia, backing out! Good girl. Did the right thing there.

He still felt cheerful when he got outside. It was a bright chilly night, lots of people on the streets, cars buzzing by. He turned the collar of his bomber jacket up, and strode along thinking of nothing in particular, but soon noticed a woman walking alone a few yards ahead of him, youngish, at least from her clothes and loose hair.

Should I? he thought, though not very clearly, for this was such a private game that he hardly admitted playing it even to himself. He deliberated, still vaguely, until she turned off the main road and headed up something lesser, less crowded, less well-lit. Right until he reached the corner himself he didn't know whether he was going to but as he

18

reached it his feet seemed to decide for him, and he turned and followed her.

Good long road. He quickened his pace a little, his hands still in his pockets. He was only fifteen feet or so behind her now. Practice had given him a certain expertise, he could have predicted the precise moment when she'd take the first quick glance over her shoulder, just to check. There. Hallo there, thought Russell, looking away. He thought of himself as she must see him, dark, his face hidden; he might be Death itself stalking her, they both knew that. Though she wasn't sure yet. She'd take another look round soon, she'd speed up, maybe cross the road to see if he'd cross it too, cross back again to make sure, they often did that, as if they just couldn't believe it at first.

Yes. She was speeding up. Heels on, tap tap tap. Russell walked faster, his heart beginning to pound. Soon she'd start running, and so would he, gaining on her easy as you like, until, within grasping distance, when he could hear her breath, he would sheer off suddenly and dash off in another direction, back to the lighted streets for a good old laugh.

Once a girl had belted off to some tower block, and actually started running up the steps, *Spiral-Staircase*-style, and he'd been so carried away he'd gone up after her, four whole flights, until she'd leant on a doorbell and he'd stopped so abruptly he'd nearly fallen over – there were boyfriends with friends and Alsatians to consider after all – and he'd shot back down again even faster than he'd come up.

This one was hobbling along well now. Russell could barely contain himself, her bottom looked so funny urgently swinging from side to side. What did they wear high heels for? She turned again, and in the lamplight he saw that she was coloured, not black but a mixture of something, coffee-coloured. The steam went out of him. Russell was always polite to the ethnic group. He slowed down, and let her go.

19

Still. Exhilarating though. The thrill of the chase. The cheek of them, imagining he'd hurt them. As if I would, he thought, as he made his way back to the main road. Wouldn't hurt a fly, me.

The people still flowed, the cars and lorries burst past them, the shop windows glowed. On the corner Russell paused, taking a deep breath. This is my time, he thought. A motorbike roared by, its glossy metal picked out in reflected light, the rider's helmet and leathers edged with gold. It was a feeling like nostalgia that gripped Russell, but a sweet nostalgia for the here and now, to which he so pleasantly belonged.

He swung off jauntily into the crowd, humming a little.

5

ONCE A MAN GOT UP EARLY FROM JANET'S BED, AND went away leaving two twenty-pound notes wedged into her hairbrush on the cluttered chest of drawers. It was a day or two before Janet noticed them, and at first she was just puzzled. How could she have forgotten such a large amount, especially when she'd somehow put it in such an unprecedented place? It was only when he didn't ring and didn't ring that light dawned and she had a few very nasty moments.

But then forty quid was forty quid, there was no point getting all hysterical about it and tearing it up or flushing it down the loo, and she could hardly send it back, not knowing his address, or his number, or his surname come to that. It had been his mistake. Besides she could barely remember him anyway, she hadn't exactly been pining.

Janet took the money to the West End and bought herself a long black stylish dress with it, but all the same it struck her how easy it would be to take up that line of work, how easy, in effect, it had been. She had not realised before how accurate the phrase 'drifting into prostitution' might actually be.

Not that forty pounds a go seemed at all fair. She remembered a chatty Welsh girl she'd met up with once or twice for drinks, who'd consorted with Arabs on a cash basis.

'Honest Jan it's two hundred a jump!' The Welsh girl had had quite poor skin as well. Two hundred a jump! In that elongated lascivious accent. 'Get you in, love, no problem, if you—'

'Oh no, thanks, I don't think so . . .' Though the idea had rather excited her at the time, she had seen herself through it, someone hard and smart, checking appointments in a leather-bound filofax, snapping shut an expensive handbag in some cool classy bar: an executive tart.

Idiotic. For me anyway, thought Janet, remembering this as she climbed into bed. She checked around, but everything still looked just as it had the day she'd moved in: neat, clean, blue rug, pine chest of drawers with a little swing mirror sitting on top, bedside table with a plain white lamp on it. And no junk of any kind, no make-up or jewellery, no Kleenex box or Tampax or loose change or hairgrips. No hairbrush. Perhaps this time it would last.

Especially with this odd new thing to do. She picked up her recorder, a plastic-topped wooden one acquired that morning along with a booklet detailing its trickier reaches, and opened the fat bookful of music.

'By the wa-a-a-aters,' she sang, softly, in case they were in downstairs, 'waters of Babylon—' Here she pointed the recorder, consulted the booklet, felt her way at length into B flat, and gently blew.

Really? Could that be right? It sounded so peculiar. Of course it was a very modern piece. But then even the Mendelssohn anthem sounded wrong sung on its own. You had to hear all the other parts along with it to make it sound – well, not like a tune, of course, but as if it had some bearing on one. You especially had to hear the soprano line. Because the sopranos always seemed to get the melody, the part that sounded natural on its own, leading along as simply as a road, going up hills and down the other side and concluding at a destination you could see in advance. Whereas the alto line just knocked about all over the place, circling at random, or backwards, and suddenly halting in precarious mid-stride on notes that sounded as if they ought to be leading up to something else, but didn't.

It's not what I remembered, thought Janet, but then a few hymns long ago, and all of them so well known, hardly counted, perhaps, as previous alto experience at all. I wish we had the tune now and then. It's not fair. They're not memorable, the other parts. They couldn't haunt you. In the bath, say, or on the bus. They're not for private use. Bit of a drawback really.

Janet picked up the recorder again and played the whole long phrase. Sounded like fish singing, she thought, sniggering, sounded like those whales that hum at length beneath the waves.

And perhaps this was all rather a waste of time really. It would be easier to sight-read it with the rest of the choir than pore over it alone. It was disappointing. She had rather counted on needing lots of practice, on having something so particular to do. She had seen herself hard at it, completely absorbed the way real musicians were, if films and books and so on were anything to go by – like Laurence in *Little Women* rushing to the piano after Jo had chucked him, and playing the *Sonata Pathétique* as never before. Though really you'd think he could have come up with something a bit more original at a time like that, or at least something a bit less like the only thing people who can't play a note can be counted on to recognise, Oh yes, pom, po-pom po-pom pom!

It tipped you off, that sort of thing, she felt. Making him play something everyone would recognise just made it obvious that he was only a made-up person in a story; a real person would surely have had a quick miserable bash at whatever was left on the music stand, and gone all wrong from being so upset anyway, and crashed the lid down and stomped off upstairs. That was what real people did. Well,

23

that's what would have happened if I'd tried it anyway, thought Janet.

She poured hot water onto a one-cup tea-bag and stood for a moment admiring her kitchen, which was spotless. There was even a bowl of oranges on one of the worktops, which was just the sort of detail they used in the magazines to give elegant perfection that homely touch. And of course loaded tea-trays on beds, she reflected, as she swung the tea-bag into the bin. Though that one always looked a bit problematical, because the bed was always beautifully made, so what could the people be playing at, deciding to have their tea in a bedroom? And then you couldn't help wondering where they'd all gone all of a sudden. What could have happened to make everyone rush off like that leaving a loaded tea-tray behind like something on the *Marie Celeste*?

Smiling, Janet stirred her tea, and as she did so became aware of a sense of contentment, of not, for the moment, wanting anything she couldn't have. For a little while she allowed herself to savour it, pretending she had every right to it, just seeing what it felt like; but it quickly turned out to feel like asking for trouble. She took the mug of tea back to the bedroom, and sat in the blue covered armchair, trying to calm herself with its empty tidiness.

At the back of Janet's mind, too far back for her to reach, were childhood picture books, and the homes of the small animals shown there, simple, uncluttered and clean, bedrooms with one bed in them and a bit of curtained window and nothing else, kitchens sketched in set for breakfast maybe but never hectic with piles of junk mail or newspapers or half-empty milk bottles.

Get the setting right, said the back of Janet's mind, and you might find the unconscious contentment of Ratty before Mole muscled in, or of the Teddy Bear Postman, who even ate his Christmas dinner on his own and seemed to have nothing to complain about. The Teddy Bear Postman never felt lonely, never lay awake at night tearing

24

himself apart with longing. He just got up and went to work and got his own supper and put the china away. Get the setting right. That's all it takes.

When the mug was empty she took it back to the kitchen, washed it, dried it, and put it away. Even so she could feel herself beginning to struggle as she climbed into bed. Humming loudly she snatched up the paperback from under the bed, found her place and, sweating now, forcibly read it, left to right, left right, left right, but it didn't work; the words fell away, and the sweet-shop doorbell tinkled, and in came the lady from the village in her smart camel coat and dark velour hat. She saw Janet at once, but kept her eyes still as she turned away, and made that movement she has been making, in memory, ever since, her hand drawing in her coat in a deliberate skirting movement to avoid contamination, small enough, hardly noticeable really. She'd asked for a box of After Eights, and the woman behind the counter had served her, though it had clearly been Janet's turn.

'Lovely morning,' the lady from the village had said, popping the box into her basket. The woman behind the counter had agreed, 'Lovely!' and the lady from the village had turned, still smiling, and gone out as if she had simply not seen anyone else, let alone shunned them.

'What was it you wanted?'

Janet could not speak. Trying to hold her raincoat together over her vast stomach with one hand she had pointed with the other at a Milky Way.

'Go on then.' The woman behind the counter, a fat pale face ringed with dull curls: 'No, love. You keep the money. Never mind her. You keep the money. Think yourself lucky, they never used to let you girls out at all. Like a prison it was.'

Janet did not even smile. She wished she had asked for a Mars bar, so much bigger, she was so hungry all the time, especially at night, sick with hunger. She took the Milky Way and lumbered off with it without a word of thanks.

Well, I felt so unclean. I felt she was right, the lady from the village. Maybe not then but ever since I saw his face—

'Aah!' cried Janet aloud, pressing her hands to her eyes—

I saw his face, and it was my own, my own remembered face, pointed chin and everything, I had never once thought the baby would look like me, I'd thought of it just as it, the disaster, the thing I had to put behind me, the unfortunate incident I would soon be able to put into perspective, who'd be going to a far better home than I could ever provide and so on and so on and so on, all that stuff I kept in my head to repeat to myself when I saw his shared face, all that stuff I let other people say to me, all that stuff I should have thrown out there and then, but I didn't, I didn't, I didn't.

Janet sat up, and picked up her book again. There was now a chance, she thought, having gone through the sweet-shop part again and taken another look at him, that she could manage to stop things there. This type of brief mauling was often enough to keep all the rest of it at bay for a while. Whereas letting it go, letting the full strength of her immense and useless regret take over and make a night of it did no good at all, made the gaps between its full-scale outbreaks shorter rather than otherwise. By now she knew its habits very well. Nothing could hold it back for ever, not travel or meditation or Jesus or yoga. Or singing, evidently. Drink often fuddled it, sometimes enraged it; the early days of love affairs saw it right off, the later ones yanked it straight back again; meeting anyone new, of either sex, gave it a strong shove forwards, what with Janet worrying about if and when to spill the beans; meeting anyone from the past emboldened it, it liked the loaded or tactful question, asked or significantly not asked at all. Most of all it liked sex, which had engendered it. Janet had liked sex once as well, and her various attempts to go on liking it had led her into a great many difficulties over the years.

She found her place in the book again. I did it, she thought clearly, for she had found this admission often helped. I did it, the worst thing, I gave him away, and it was all my own doing and all my own fault.

There. Hear that?

This time, reading, the words made sense. It was a thin paperback, lent her by a friend. She had no idea who wrote it or what its title was, but at least all the things in it were happening to someone else. Sad things too. Janet liked that.

6

ON WEDNESDAY EVENING ANNIE WENT ROUND TO visit her sister, taking a bunch of freesias and that month's *Cosmopolitan*.

'Someone at work gave it to me,' she said, as she followed Marion along the dark, cluttered passage. She felt very uneasy telling this lie, as she had not planned to, had just imagined herself handing over these little presents as a matter of course, needing no comment. As if Marion was in hospital, she now saw, or in prison. And it was no use hoping Marion wouldn't have noticed; spotting underlying assumptions was a hobby of hers. Or had been.

'How's that boy?' asked Annie, to speed things out of the danger zone.

'Oh, he's fine, he's terrific actually, he walked halfway across the kitchen this morning, he was so pleased with himself, he was laughing and laughing.'

'Is he sleeping, though?'

'There.' Marion set the little vase of freesias on the table. 'They're nice, thanks. Is he sleeping? No he's not. Not so's you'd notice,' she said, without rancour. 'Want some coffee?'

'Yes please. You're looking well though.' This routine lie, told to comfort them both, gave neither any trouble.

'I feel better,' said Marion, fishing about in the sink for mugs. 'I'm getting out a bit more.' She looked about for a tea-towel, gave up, and shook the mugs briefly before pressing them dry against her jumper. 'Sorry about the mess. Did it smell funny when you came in?'

Annie shrugged. 'Just Dettol. Muff at it again?'

'I don't know what to do with him. It's obviously something to do with Lewis, he's jealous or something.'

'I didn't think cats were like that. Not if you've had them done anyway.' Privately Annie thought Muff was more a symptom than a pet, that putting up with his various horrible habits was yet more evidence that Marion had some neurotic compulsion to make her life as dreary and uncomfortable as possible.

'And all this is Benny,' said Marion, gesturing at the trio of black plastic bin-liners slouched in a corner. 'He's been having a clear-out; he was supposed to take them to Oxfam.'

'Oh, is he out?'

'Yes. I made him. I said you were coming.'

'Oh, thanks!'

'No, you know what I mean. He knew I wouldn't be on my own. He's seeing some old mate of his. The old days, you know.'

Annie sat down at the kitchen table.

'How's, er—' she glanced up at the ceiling. 'Is it working out?'

'I think so. She's ever so quiet. I hardly see her; she goes straight up and shuts the door. You'd hardly know she was there.'

'Sounds ideal.'

'Well, I hope so. I mean, I hope she's all right up there. We've hardly spoken since she moved in. She said she couldn't hear Lewis – I did ask. I can't hear her at all. I think she takes her shoes off.'

'Gawd,' said Annie, slightly disgusted. Wasn't this taking

consideration rather too far? Creeping about, she thought. 'What does she do anyway?'

'She's a nurse,' said Marion, rather defensively, for she had chosen her tenant over several other possibles.

And past thirty, Annie remembered. Renting on her own, and being a nurse, and slipping off her shoes; I bet she thinks of it as slipping them off. For a moment Annie saw the lodger quite clearly, fat and fluttery, a breathy giggler with carefully feminine clothes, flowery skirts and fluffy jumpers with pictures of animals knitted into them, blu-tacking wrapping paper with kittens and puppies and so forth on it up on her bedroom walls, and making soft toys for a hobby, and trapunto cushion covers and ruffled curtains, and yet somehow being rather a neuter all the same. The picture was so vivid that Annie did not look at it too closely, though if she had she might have recognised her own cousin Felicity, whose portrait it was.

(Felicity's mother had married money, and sent her children to private schools; once or twice she had sent on parcels of Felicity's outgrown summer dresses, all smart and pretty with various Knightsbridge labels inside.

'But just look at the size of them!'

Marion and Annie had been quite shocked by their own mother's scornful glee. Mothers in books never sniggered or said, 'What a whopper!' That was the sort of thing mothers ought gently to chide their children for, not vigorously do themselves. But of course it was no use pointing out these little errors of taste, and anyway both of them had known that any minute now mum was going to stop being angrily amused and turn plain nasty, shouting 'Bloody cast-offs! Who does she think she is!' and letting everyone else in for a day or so of behaviour that in any child would have been labelled The Sulks.)

'She sounds rather awful,' said Annie now, without any idea where her disapproval came from. Certainly relations between the cousins had been painfully stiff and embarrassing during their occasional childhood visits. Though in recent years Annie in particular had been quite pleased to meet up with old Felicity now and then, perfectly nice after all, and so fat, so breathy, so bored, poor thing, Health Visiting in Tunbridge Wells.

'She's okay,' said Marion at the fridge. 'She's just a bit distant, that's all. She's ever so small. She hardly comes up to my shoulder. She left a pair of jeans drying in the bathroom yesterday, I couldn't think whose they were, they looked like a child's.' They had given her rather a pang, she remembered. Absurd. Something to do with motherhood, presumably. A tenderness overflow, altogether drippy. 'And she's Scottish. D'you ever get this, I mean whenever I'm talking to her I have to make a real effort not to talk back like it, you know put her accent on, it's sort of automatic . . . not that we've talked that much, you know, she's a bit, like I say, distant.'

None of this fitted cousin Felicity in the least. Scottish? Distant? Annie frowned, almost puzzled.

'Gave me six months rent in advance though,' said Marion.

'Ah. Well, that's the important thing I suppose.' Annie swung her handbag onto her lap, pulled out her cigarettes. 'How did Sunday go, anyway?'

'Oh. The usual. Well. Worse actually.' Marion sat down too.

'Oh?'

'Yeah, we were late. Honestly, about ten minutes. Not fifteen – ten or eleven minutes.'

'What, and there was a row?'

'Sort of, I mean there's never actually a row—'

Benny's father had opened the door himself, immediately. He had flung it open:

'Oh, so you've come then!'

'I mean,' said Marion now, 'I didn't know what he was on about for a moment – if you've crossed half London, being ten minutes late, well, it doesn't occur to you. I said, "Sorry?" And his mum's there peeping out, she's got this little smirk on. And Benny starts saying, "Oh, well, we nearly ran out of petrol, we had to find a garage—"'

'Oh dear.'

'Yes, he just hit the roof, he just leapt, What d'you think you're doing looking for garages, dragging a baby all over the place looking for garages on a Sunday, why hadn't he checked earlier, why wouldn't he learn, why was he such a hopeless useless piece of rubbish—'

'No!'

'Yes. That's what he said. I mean it's always like that, there's always something. Anyway. We were just standing there. I said to Benny, "Come on, let's go home." And I turned round, started walking back to the car. And he runs down the steps, he bounced, Ben's dad, "Oh where are you going? You've only just come, don't be in such a hurry, you mustn't mind me." All jocular. And his mum nips down in her slippers, "Oh Benny love, how lovely to see you all and the little man, ooh let me hold him—"'

'Yuk.'

'Yes. You should have seen Benny's face. All stiff. But not angry. He doesn't get angry. That's what I'm for, I get angry for him.'

There was a pause.

'So then what happened? You all went in?'

'Yeah.'

'And no one said anything.'

'Nope. Everyone nice as pie. You know, nice happy family cooing over the baby. And Benny in on it. I wouldn't mind, but he won't so much as look at me. No signal, like, We're in this together. Nothing. Because we're not.'

'Well. You know what I think.'

Marion sighed.

'You're going to let Lewis see all that? He's not going to stay a baby, is he?'

'I couldn't cope on my own.'

'I'd be there, I'd help you.'

'Not every night. Not in the mornings. He cries so much,

32

I get so tired. I forgot the coffee,' said Marion distractedly, getting up.

'For all we know it's affecting him already,' said Annie angrily. Her sensations while saying this, the stiffening about her mouth and throat, the faint roaring in her ears, told her clearly that she was being cruel. It's for her own good, she told herself, but her heart beat faster. She felt a little tinge as well of ancient apprehension. Marion was the elder. Once long ago she had bolted Annie into an abandoned henhouse where Annie had howled and scrabbled for what seemed like hours before, much scratched by chicken wire, she had desperately forced her way out through the hens' own tiny Gothic archway.

'Sorry,' said Annie presently, meaning: That was just force of habit, a leftover from the old days, I withdraw it.

'He was asleep the whole time actually,' said Marion, busy with spoons and instant coffee, meaning: Sounded like a give-away to me, revealing your true position, same old arch-rival, enemy at heart.

There had been a slight wobble to Marion's voice as well, which had further added: And after all that has happened!

Hell, hell, thought Annie in distress, having heard all this loud and clear. There was a short silence, while she cast about her for a diversion.

'Oh, can I see him? It's ages, I mean over a week since I—'

'If you like. Don't wake him up though.' Marion switched the kettle on again.

Not coming with me then, thought Annie, hanging about hopefully for a moment or two. She gave up and crossed the landing. The baby's room was tiny, hardly big enough for a bed, the sort of room that looks accidental, as if the architect had been as surprised and nonplussed by it as all its tenants since. Cosy for a cot though, thought Annie, stealthily approaching. Under his sensory bombardment of musical mobiles, interesting shapes in tinfoil and plastic sheep on elastic, Lewis looked, even to Annie, simply

33

delicious, his skin translucent, his fingers splayed palm-down in the utter relaxation only babies can achieve.

As she tiptoed out Marion was standing in the doorway. On the landing they embraced, a little clumsily, as Marion was holding two full mugs.

'Sorry,' said Marion into Annie's shoulder. 'I'm just so on edge.'

'Nothing to apologise for,' said Annie, reflecting that this was indeed the case, that their disagreement had been entirely implied. She is apologising for the set of her shoulders at the sink, thought Annie; she is apologising for feelings she almost didn't show at all. I'm glad I've got her, I'm glad I've got a sister. This seemed such an odd, simple conclusion that she smiled at it. She suddenly felt rather cheerful altogether.

'How's that Peter, then?' asked Marion invitingly, back in the kitchen, and Annie smiled. For the previous evening, despite the wrecked weekend, had gone off very well, all of them somehow in good spirits; Peter had been loving, Joe had turned out to have done something at work that he was especially pleased about (poor old Joe, whatever was it that he actually did?), Peter had made them both laugh and laugh—

'He's got this new boss,' said Annie, grinning. She started on a description of Peter's latest ultimate superior at Whitehall, a mandarin known as God-Awful, whose minions, from Peter himself down to the lowest, dimmest, gawping clerical were, according to Peter, so generally overcome by his unique combination of reptilian appear-ance, wet-handed smarminess and loose-lipped, dry-mouthed speech defect that they were unable to communi-cate privately with one another in anything but God-Awful take-offs. At lunchtime whole tablesful of gesticulating God-Awfuls sneeringly passed one another the salt or nasally brayed about last night's *Eastenders*. It was a God-Awful epidemic, Peter had claimed, doing God-Awful peering into his beer, and trying to open a packet of crisps, and (not actually that amusing really, Annie had thought at the time) being God-Awful frenziedly struggling out of his clothes in Annie's bedroom later on that night.

'Like this,' said Annie, doing an impression of Peter doing one, and of someone she had never actually seen. Marion still laughed. Once, when she was pregnant and sick and discouraged, Peter had come round with Annie to visit, and done Mrs Thatcher in apocalyptic rage, not just accurately, but at fierce and articulate length, and Marion had laughed so much she had had to go and lie down.

'He's so talented,' she sighed now, smiling.

'Yeah,' said Annie.

'He's a charmer.'

'He's a mess.' Working tonight, he said. As ever. Unavailable until Friday night, and possibly not then.

'We're on the verge,' said Annie.

'Oh?'

'Yes,' said Annie, and began.

7

'NICE TO SEE YOU EAT,' SAID STANLEY, USING another of Amy's phrases.

Peter, his mouth full, barely twitched. Instead he gave the sort of minimal friendly shrug with which he would have answered his mother. 'Looking a bit peaky.' We'd had that one as well tonight, he thought. While he was hanging my coat up. That had been the first one too, come to think of it, what, barely a month after the funeral?

'Looking a bit peaky.' Peter had held his breath then, imagining that Stanley was doing it on purpose, or at least consciously, in some ham-fisted attempt at consolation, at being mum as well as dad. But Stanley hadn't caught his eye, or grimaced or checked himself in any way. Hadn't noticed, hadn't heard himself at all, and that was flaming typical, Peter had thought to himself, momentarily enraged.

For a while he'd gone on cringing, month after month, while Stanley would come up with more and more of the things Amy used to say, and seem perfectly unconscious about saying them himself.

'Why are you doing this?' Peter had several times imagined himself furiously demanding. It was somehow impossible to imagine asking lightly or gently.

'Why are you doing this?' Yes, only a snarl would come out, no matter how he rehearsed it. And:

'—doing what?' his poor old dad would ask back, all innocence.

'. . . am I?'

'. . . really?'

'. . . oh . . . sorry . . . I hadn't realised . . .'

And then what, he'd look away, he'd look down, look all tired and shrivelled, poor old sod. No. Out of the question. Just put up with it, Peter had told himself. But sometimes, all the same, his eyes had ached. It was surprising how many phrases there were.

Fly cuppa?

She's no spring chicken.

Up the wooden hill.

Good lad.

Dozens of them, and their repetition, in someone else's mouth, had the effect, not of bringing his mother closer, but its opposite, of distancing her and making her somehow less vivid. He was inclined to blame her, parroting away like that. And his father too, for showing her up. For a while he had stayed away, inventing all sorts of reasons for himself and for Stanley as to why he was too busy even for one evening every month or so in his father's company.

'I dunno, I can't stand it,' he had told Annie as they lay in bed one night. 'I didn't even know she was doing it.'

'What, saying the same thing all the time? We all do it. You do, I do. We just use the current phrases, not elderly-lady ones. They stick out more when they're old.'

Peter had closed his eyes, listening but discontented. Yeah, that's all very well, he wanted to say, but—

But I don't really care about that. Not really. Since he was unwilling to say quite what it was that he really cared about he kept quiet, for suspecting his father of an uncon-scious design – a nasty attempt to belittle his mother, as he had on occasion sneered at and bullied her when she was alive, and out of some mean marital habit – was too

37

shamefully painful to look at properly and name, to himself or anyone else. He felt impatient, Annie rabbiting on.

'See, they're like clothes, fashion, the things we repeat. And not obvious until they're really out, I mean, I hardly notice what you wear, it's unremarkable, but I'd notice' – Annie grinned – 'if you turned up in flares, I'd see them straight away.'

'Yeah.'

'They tell people something about you, phrases, like clothes. But not everything. Not that much. They're what, accessories. Like her gloves, or her handbag. They aren't her, they're not summing her up. They're just accessories.'

Ah. Peter had turned that one over. Accessories?

'He just misses her, that's all.'

Yes, thought Peter, I can see that's what it would look like, to anyone else.

All the same he had called round on Stanley a few days later and found it mysteriously less painful, if he braced himself. Her old handbag, he told himself. Her gloves.

'Nice to see you eat.' Almost used to it now.

'It's very good,' said Peter, swallowing. The pastry melted in the mouth, the meat fell lusciously apart. Cooking like her too these days. Competing with her.

'I might just be imagining it,' he'd suggested to Annie lately.

'Why should you be?'

'Work going well?' This, at least, was Stanley's own old territory.

'Yeah, very well, thanks.'

'Do you mind, then?'

'No. Too greedy.'

'The new boss not so bad then?'

'Oh . . . he's all right . . .' Peter sounded vague, hoping to deflect any further questions. Stanley had been so pleased when he'd started at Whitehall, a real job at last, pay, prospects, fast promotion. Pension. He'd been all congratulatory and thrilled, still was, still asking eager questions when for years, informed say of Chapter Three's sudden burst of speed, or Professor X's encouraging remarks, or a respectful mention of P. Laidlaw in someone else's parallel investigations, he had merely grunted, and turned back to the *Daily Mail*.

His mother, Peter thought, would have been more understanding, or at any rate more tactful. She would have hidden some of her pleasure, knowing to what extent the job, for all its glowing future, was really a capitulation. Not that I've given up, thought Peter, though rather on automatic, far from it, not at all.

I wish I'd got the job before she died though. In a way. She'd been so worried. That Dennis. That Mike. Her sister Bea's boys, cropping up in conversation now and then, buying their own houses, getting bigger cars, producing grandchildren; and dad so careful to let me know that time Dennis took Bea off to Corfu for a fortnight, and when he paid to have her sodding bungalow re-wired, and when Mike bought her a knitting machine for Christmas.

And mum sticking up for me.

'Corfu,' Amy had sniffed. 'Free baby-sitting, more like.' And she'd told them Bea was driving everyone mad with jumpers, that everyone Bea knew was being bombarded with enormous great acrylic jumpers she kept zipping off on her machine, she was obsessed with it, stuck at it day and night rattling them out all shapes and sizes—

I gave her a basket of things from the Body Shop that year. Not even a big basket. Her last Christmas. Not that anyone knew that. I wish I'd got the job before she died.

For a moment Peter saw her unwrapping the vast, gleaming, what did they look like anyway? knitting machine, saw her delight,

'Oh, son, oh thanks, love!'

'Annie all right?' Stanley asked.

'What, sorry?' Peter put up a hand, and pushed back his hair.

'Annie, all right, is she?'

'Oh, yeah, she's fine thanks.'

'And Joe, how's he getting on these days, is he, you know, seeing anyone?'

'No. He's okay though. No: he's doing very well actually. He's just finished a paper for *Nature*, it's going to establish him.'

Stanley nodded. The last part was clear enough. How to get past the first bit? He pondered.

'What, it's going to be published, then, is it?'

This seemed to fit well enough.

'Well, it's off for review. You know, other experts in the field have a look at it, say what they think, let *Nature* know.

Let nature know? Frowning, Stanley began collecting the plates together, deciding on one last try.

'Is he still working with that chap? The Oxford one?'

'Yeah, I think so—'

It happened that a month or so earlier a very nice young lady doctor had mentioned the Oxford chap by name, after a lecture on plant research at Stanley's gardening club, and Stanley had told her about Joe, his son's oldest friend, who worked with this chap, and she'd been really impressed, had since treated him, Stanley, with a certain extra respect and politeness, as if he must clearly be a rather more interesting person than she'd first taken him for, and all for being related to a friend of someone who worked with Whateverhisnamewas in Oxford.

It had been enlightening, and disconcerting. Had he not been inclined to scoff at this Joe himself, still living like a student when Peter at least had had the sense to clear out and get a proper job? Once or twice too he had blamed Joe, for influencing Peter; the two of them had clearly been propping one another up in this endless and profitless so-called researching.

That GP's eyes had fairly popped though. Impressed, and a doctor! Stanley had worried a little ever since. Perhaps after all he had been quite wrong, had simply not known enough about the structure of the world. Perhaps, out of ignorance, he had been of no help to his child.

'No, I'll wash, you dry,' said Peter, following Stanley into the kitchen.

Stanley took up the tea-cloth. 'You still, you know, carrying on with your other work?' he asked diffidently.

The look Peter turned on him, simple surprise, spoke directly to the worry: Yes. You were no help at all.

'Oh, well. Yes, when I can. Still some way to go though.'

He started washing up, crashing things about rather a lot in the sink.

'Here, steady on, that's her best china you've—'

'Yes, yes, sorry,' said Peter, all clenched.

Thoughtless, careless, thought Stanley, but at the same time he was a little uncomfortable, and did the rest of the drying-up almost in slow-motion, to prove to them both that he had been prompted by real reverence for his dead wife's china; while Peter scrubbed hard at the pie dish, showing his father his answer: Any opportunity, you just can't pass it up, can you, you've just got to get in there and nag, nag, nag—

At last Stanley thought of something safe to say. 'So. What's Joe going to do with himself now?'

Peter gave a little sigh of relief, for after years of furious pleasure in combat he now found disagreements with his father mysteriously hard to bear. 'Oh,' he said quite cheerfully, 'he's got lots of ideas from his results. You see, he's—' and he embarked on an account of what Joe had been up to; risky in any other company, as Peter could not understand several aspects of Joe's research, and was thus unable to remember various important details, so that anyone with, say, 'A' level physics could have stumped him instantly with a simple question or two.

As it was, Stanley was soon happy to stop listening altogether, to relax and just watch Peter talk. Waving his hands about exactly like his mother, thought Stanley. He remembered coming upon Amy and Bea arguing once, he'd seen Bea reach out and hold Amy's hand still, the better to get a word of her own in edgeways; it had worked too.

'So, he used these radioactive isotopes . . .'

And after all it was companionable, washing up together. I'd've been in the sitting-room, thought Stanley vaguely. She'd've been in here talking to him while I looked at the crossword. He could remember it now, their voices rising and falling, a laugh sometimes, or the radio on.

'. . . and he plotted these other results against his graphs and they made sense; this other bloke had got the data, you see, but misinterpreted it. Practically got it upside-down!'

Peter laughed, turning to his father, and Stanley smiled back, as if he had understood.

'Now. You staying for a cuppa?'

Mum again, thought Peter, hanging up the dishcloth. Carefully he spread it over the taps to dry, as he always had for his mother.

'Yeah, lovely. Thanks.'

'Good lad,' said Stanley.

8

ONCE LONG AGO, A THERAPIST HAD TOLD JOE TO look at Annabel's photographs, to make a point of it, daily. Joe had liked the therapist and wanted to please her, so he had ended up making quite a performance of it, going straight into his living room every night to look at the framed portrait on the mantelpiece, then off to the bedroom for the bedside-table one, and finally back to the passage where he'd left his briefcase, for a quick hard look at the plastic-wallet one tucked into the inside flap.

'Just don't let them take you by surprise.' Nor had they now, for five or six years: Annabel smiling from beneath a broad-brimmed straw hat, Annabel sitting at a table under a sign reading CAFÉ TABAC, Annabel naked in a stream somewhere in the Howgills, her breasts hidden beneath her arm, not by design but by graceful accident, smiling again, about to splash him.

Hallo there. Hallo there. Hallo.

Lately Joe had worked out a theory of his own about Annabel. It was something to do with Annie, he thought, and the way she always treated him as Peter's friend. Like someone in a cast list: *Joe, research physicist, Peter's friend.* That's what I am, Joe told himself. I'm supporting cast. I wasn't meant for a big part, I'm not cut out for it. Annabel was. You just had to look at her to see she was the real thing, the heroine, the one the whole plot turned around. And she somehow hadn't noticed that he, Joe, was actually only the bloke at the back carrying a spear in Act One, or the nameless crewman who beams down with Mr Spock and the Captain, and gets zapped by alien life-forms in the first ten minutes.

Thinking of this Joe gave a small snorting laugh. It's all your fault, Annabel. Getting into the wrong sub-plot. You were just too much for me. He sighed. He felt restless tonight. He got up, stretching, and joints cracked in his neck and elbows. For a moment he stood still, considering, then went to the telephone and dialled.

'Hallo, Frances?'

'Yes, hallo?'

'Hallo, it's Joe Tate. How are you?'

That sound she made; he could just see her shrugging.

'I, ah, have to be in Cambridge tomorrow. I was wondering if I could come over?'

'Um. When?'

'About eight?'

'Should be all right. But I'll be going out at nine.'

'Good. Right then. Look forward to it,' said Joe politely, but she only laughed and hung up.

Joe went and turned the taps on for a bath, whistling through his teeth, self-consciously. He was aware of his reflection in the mirror on the bathroom cabinet; it was like someone hovering, trying to catch his eye and get a word in. Eventually he straightened up, faced it, mentally told it to sod off, and put the radio on. Voices rose with the steam, blurring, enveloping.

The bath soon filled. Listening carefully, Joe climbed in.

9

THE SECOND TENORS WERE STILL GETTING IT WRONG, even with the accompanyist thumping out the line in double octaves.

'No, no, no, la la la LA, Dorothy, would you—'

The rest of the choir was beginning to fidget and mutter; it was just like being back at school, thought Janet, recognising the atmosphere of mingled tension and boredom.

'There's always trouble with tenors,' whispered the elderly lady to Janet's right.

Janet smiled. Trouble with tenors. She saw them, neat in their beige cardigans, rowdily breaking bottles and kicking the seats in front of them.

'Most men want to sing bass,' the elderly lady went on. 'Think it's more manly, probably. Anyway there's never enough tenors to go round, so standards tend to slip, you see.'

She seemed, thought Janet, rather different from the other elderly ladies of the choir, who were faintly menacing as a rule, well-groomed and well-upholstered, moneyed, perfumed and intransigent.

Behind them the straining voices hit another set of clashing variants.

'Crummy lot,' whispered the old lady.

Janet wanted very much to say something normal and friendly back in reply, but a familiar lock seemed to have turned in her brain, so that several moments passed before she thought of 'Have you sung in many choirs?' Shyness also made her run so many pre-speech normality-and-friendliness checks that the words became impossible to say naturally, became a public announcement, fraught with terrors; by this time the moment for saying them was well past anyway.

'Once more, listen once more—'

Robert was almost bullying them now, exasperated, while the second tenors, that little band of lost sheep, were clearly running round in panicky circles, coming up with new ways of getting it all wrong, uttering discordant bleats while their short-tempered collie snapped at their ankles.

'I don't know who he thinks he's dealing with,' hissed the old lady, disapproving; 'I mean, they are paying for this. It's supposed to be for pleasure,' she added, almost in normal tones, and one or two answering murmurs arose in agreement around her.

'Funny really,' she went on, whispering to Janet, 'funny business all round really. I mean, all of us actually pay more, per person, to sing, than the audience does to listen to us. Don't you think that's odd?'

Janet could only blink; this aspect of concert-going had not occurred to her.

'Mind you, it's probably only fair. We obviously enjoy ourselves a great deal more than the audience does.'

At this, and at Janet's breathy giggle, one or two altos in the row in front briefly turned round, their faces perfectly polite and neutral, but in plain rebuke all the same, for too much mid-rehearsal chat was against the rules.

Janet's response was automatic and unconscious. Her hard mouth and insolent eyes said straight away:

Who you looking at?

46

and the front-line altos dropped their eyes and whipped their heads back round again, evidently chilled.

Janet, after a second or so's fierce satisfaction, saw that she had betrayed herself, acted the snarling underdog when all that had been required or expected was lowered eyes. I just don't know how to behave, she thought, I'm either struck dumb or picking fights, it's always the same—

Luckily at this point Robert took out a handkerchief, wiped his forehead, and let the tenors off the hook for the moment, and Janet, getting to her feet with everyone else, saw that this bit, the next bit, was her favourite, calling for a great deal of *fortissimo* and all within her range. Great happiness seized her as she sang. It was a feeling of smooth cleanliness within, of lightness, of being beyond concentration, of being, as the piece ended, the sound itself.

'I often think of it at concerts,' said the elderly lady as they waited in the queue by the coffee-urn a little later, 'my name is Viola Downely by the way, Viola—'

'Janet—' said Janet, blushing.

'I often think, there we all are, each with our modicum of talent, organising ourselves, getting ourselves together to pay to sing; and employing people much more talented than ourselves – the orchestra, the soloists. The conductor, of course. Well actually Robert is rather out of our league altogether, far too good for us, we won't keep him long, we've caught him on the way up, as it were, though that's still no excuse for him getting quite so cross, then again his wife is supposed to have had twins recently, did you know that? Which might be enough to make anyone short-tempered. But he still has it, perfect pitch, how can he tell when one soprano is half a tone out? He can: I couldn't. And this is the real difference, do you take sugar? that he can hear not only what we are singing, but how we ought to be singing it. That is what the conductor is for: to put into words a difference in musical sound, and that is actually much more difficult than it might seem. Since it requires so much improvisation.'

'I didn't know,' said Janet carefully after a pause, 'I didn't actually know that we paid him.'

'Well, he wouldn't do it just for love,' said Mrs Downely, biting a digestive in two. 'We're the ones who do it for love, pay to do it for love. We're his third choir, too, so I'm told.'

'I hadn't thought about it at all. I mean, I've been to concerts, but I've never thought about who was putting them on. I suppose I thought the concert hall.'

'Other way round, of course; we hire the hall. But we are lucky, in a way, I always think. Much luckier, say, than mildly talented amateur actors. Or think of the sheer ghastliness of watching mildly talented amateur dancers! We may be merely background, we may just provide the scaffolding, as it were, but we are mildly talented amateur singers, and so we can be part of the highest art.'

At this Janet was immediately embarrassed, and looked away, and presently Mrs Downely excused herself and stumped off to the Ladies. She had quite a bad limp, Janet saw.

She put her paper cup in the bin and went back to her seat. She thought of the happiness of singing her best, which was so magnified by harmony with other voices. She had so far put it down to the beauty of the music; she knew that it was beautiful, especially the easier bits. But was the happiness due in fact to Art, did you feel the happiness because there was real Art about?

She remembered singing in the church choir when she was fourteen and proudly managing the alto line in Stainer's *Crucifixion*; a late Friday night rehearsal, in winter, the windows all dark, the church too, only the nave lit, where they were singing the quartet, 'God so loved the world'. The empty church had seemed to fill with the sound, returning her own emotional light vibrato:

> That he gave his only begotten son,
> That whoso believeth, believeth in Him

> Should not perish, should not perish
> But have everlasting life!

And after the last long note there had been an echoing silence, a special vibrating silence that was full of music, as if the silence following the sound were an essential part of the music, written in.

But I'd never heard it before, thought Janet, remembering it. Or since, for it hadn't happened at the actual concert later on. Perhaps the church had to be empty, perhaps it had just been a technical thing, due to the resonance of the arched empty roof.

Or perhaps, like the happiness, that strange glowing silence was the confirmation of Art. You might say so if you were Viola Downely and a bit cracked. You'd sneer if you were my dad, you'd probably want to spit . . .

But then he'd never felt that happiness, nor heard the silence. It was just one more thing the miserable old bastard would have known absolutely nothing about.

She remembered walking home after that Friday rehearsal hoping, being fourteen, that God Himself had been listening in that night, and that it was His pleasure that had made the silence quiver. What would Mrs Downely say to that? The odd thing was that Janet could imagine actually asking her, and imagine also that, however jokily (just to be on the safe side) she put it, Mrs Downely would not laugh.

But didn't I shut the door in her face just now? I let my dad shut it for me.

'What did you mean just now?' She had not intended to sound quite so abrupt, almost aggressive; but Mrs Downely, who had noted the way Janet had glared at the boring front-line altos, was charmed.

Positively a yob, she thought, greedily.

The conductor picked up his baton.

Mrs Downely smiled. 'I will tell you next week,' she said.

10

LEWIS HAD WOKEN AT ELEVEN, ONE, TWO-TWENTY, four, and, finally for the day, at half past six. Rather a worse night than usual, but not by much. Marion, who had taken even longer to get back to sleep each time than Lewis had, lay now in the armchair beside the gas fire, limply holding an empty mug. She would have liked another coffee, but that would mean walking across the room and behind Lewis, currently asleep in his pushchair.

Not worth the risk, thought Marion. If only he'd wake up cooing now and then. But it always looks like a nightmare, even if I've got him in my arms.

Anyway I'm not going there again. What was the point of a post-natal support group if it made you feel not just unsupported but nearer coming to bits? I'll give it a miss next week. It's not just that they're all bigger than he is. It was that one with the earrings, the teacher, Amanda's mummy. I can only ever remember the babies' names. Lewis's mummy, that's me.

Amanda's mummy had been late today, hurried in earrings swinging, 'Honestly she just wouldn't wake up!'

Amanda's mummy had stayed in bed too, until nearly ten. 'Oh, she always sleeps through till eight, but this was ridiculous!' A fat baby, this Amanda, rosy-cheeked, and walking early.

A tear, just the one, rolled down Marion's cheek. She let it.

Should I try to get some sleep?

They all urged her to, kindly, encouragingly, the health visitors, the doctors: Sleep when he does!

Fine if he ever napped for more than twenty minutes. And there are some things you can't do with a baby strapped on your back, wash your hair, say, or clean the bathroom.

Oh, leave the housework for a bit, you look after yourself! They tended to say that as well.

Yes, but this morning I picked up the frying pan still thick with last night's grease, and it had paw-prints in it. A little trail of mousefeet, with a weeny furrowed skid-mark to show where the beast had slipped, and right in the middle a clear impress of fur, an entire mouse-print where it had fallen over sideways, you could practically see it lying there all dazed and covered in bacon fat. And it's all still out there waiting for me. Whatever would Hannah's mummy say to that?

'D'you know these days I find I have to wash the kitchen floor twice a day,' Hannah's mummy had confided to the group that morning, 'you know, now Hannah's crawling and into everything—'

Actually Hannah's mummy was too much for everyone, really. Be fair, Marion thought. Everyone looked a bit sick at that, not just me.

But little Andy was sleeping through the night now. And that porky one with the teeth.

'Lewis just doesn't seem to need sleep at all!' Smiling, smiling, in case they all thought she was cracking up and liable to bash him one.

Which I am. Aren't I? Honest to God I felt like bashing him last night. Bawling like that. What's he got to cry for?

'Slept through till eight, and then just lay there singing to herself!'

Marion had exchanged a little look, then, with Georgie's

mummy. Georgie was still a night screamer too. But even Georgie wasn't that much comfort, being so much bigger than Lewis, and greedy and curly-haired. Beside him Lewis looked all wan and bald.

'Have you tried him with cheese?' Georgie's mother had asked.

'Made him sick,' said Marion, but nodding, smiling, to show that she was grateful for any advice from more successful mothers.

'Goat's milk?'

'He just wouldn't.'

The health visitor kept suggesting mashed beetroot. 'With potato.' Marion had felt quite sullen about it the third time. Bet you've never eaten it, she'd thought crossly. Lewis certainly hadn't.

'What on earth's this?' Benny had asked, coming upon the saucepan and poking at the mess inside with a teaspoon. And all those purple splodges on the walls—

'The only thing he really wants is breast-milk.'

Not baby-food, cheap or health-shop kind; not home-made wholemeal rusks or the sugary store-bought ones; not cow's milk, soya milk, SMA or Cow-and-Gate; not Marmite fingers, mashed banana, mashed potato, yoghurt; not any kind of meat or fish; not currant buns, peanut butter, Coco-pops, or baked beans.

'Have you tried mashed avocado?'

'Yes, but—'

('What the hell's this?' Benny had asked, holding up Lewis's bunny plate full of slimy brownish sludge.)

'—he just wouldn't.' Nodding, smiling.

Perhaps if he ate he would sleep as well. 'But not necessarily.' That was the beetroot health visitor, brightly smirking. 'No guarantee, I'm afraid.'

Perhaps if he ate and slept he wouldn't be ill all the time either, sticky eyes, ear infections, chest infections, gastro-enteritis, nappy-rash.

'It does seem a bit hard when he's breast-fed, doesn't it?'

the health visitor had cheerfully agreed. 'Still. All perfectly normal you know. Nothing to worry about.'

God no, only a real neurotic would worry about her kid being white and skinny and insomniac and anorexic and two inches shorter than all the other babies in her sodding post-natal support group, right?

Marion, limp in the armchair, gave a sudden snorting giggle, for anger often struck her as comical, especially her own. The sound was quite enough for Lewis, who, she turned in time to see, began to cry even before he opened his eyes.

'Come on then. Poor old baby. Poor old thing.' Murmuring tenderly, Marion unstrapped him, and carried him over to the armchair, and calmed him with a little feed.

'You're fixated,' she told him. His eyes sometimes made her hold her breath, so extraordinarily beautiful were they, sunny-May-sky colour. Where on earth had he got them from? Not from her, boring hazel; nor from Benny, dark brown velvet, so beautiful, she had once thought, so tender. So drearily beseeching now. So doggy. Lewis stared up at her as he sucked. Every so often, suckling him gave Marion a very pleasant sensation in her lower abdomen, fleeting, delicious, vaguely sexual.

'What, like, you know, coming?' Annie there. Doubtful, curious, and, Marion suspected, rather repelled.

'No. More like, just afterwards. No build-up.'

'A reward, then. You know, evolution. To keep you at it.'

You could almost hear her thinking: 'Yuk.'

'Well I've no objection,' Marion told Lewis. 'I just want you to eat something else as well. All right?'

Lavishly, the baby smiled. Lapis lazuli his eyes, thought Marion. His skin warm ivory.

She smiled back. 'Baldy,' she said.

11

TONIGHT FOR NOW PETER WAS ON HIS OWN. HE HELD a copy of the *Guardian* in front of him, and managed now and then to read some of it, though every so often a sort of mental trembling rose up within him, and made him too aware of himself to take the words in. His eyes went on reading though, so that when the trembling went away again he would find himself a surprising paragraph or two out of synch. He felt rather indignant about this, as if the newspaper was impatiently refusing to wait for him on purpose.

'Eh? What?' he muttered to it, almost out loud. He gave the *Guardian* a little irritated shake, and a couple approaching the table beside his decided in unison on a corner elsewhere.

Peter saw them go. I shouldn't have done it, he thought with something like panic, and his hand went up, as if all by itself, to touch the bristles that were all the hairdresser had left behind.

'Are you quite sure?' he'd asked. Peter's reflection beforehand. His own had worn a smarmy grin.

'Absolutely,' Peter had said coldly.

I must have been mad, thought Peter now. It felt nice enough, like fur. But—

Work had been a nightmare. It had been quite fun at first, and a perfect diversion, all sorts of people failing to recognise him and doing ludicrous double-takes in corridors. Wherever he went his haircut had dominated all conversation. By mid-afternoon he had begun to feel rather taken over by it, a haircut on legs; the haircut had chaired the Finance Sub-Committee, he felt, and later it completely disrupted Personnel Health Policy.

And he had to admit that, almost to a man and woman, the usual response was the complete thumbs-down.

'God, Pete, you look vicious!'

'What a thug!'

'Oh Peter,' (apparently genuine distress here, from Helga in Accounts, poor old Helga) 'but you used to be so handsome, such pretty hair, oh dear, sorry—'

'Have you, ah, had a craniotomy, Peter?'

'Erm, no, sir—'

'Because if you have, I think I should point out that the department should have been informed, so that proper sick-leave arrangements could have been made.'

'Yes, sir.'

'In fact I was under the impression that a quite lengthy stay in hospital was required, following such a serious operation.'

'It's just a haircut, sir.'

'Come now, there's no need for these foolish heroics. You get yourself back to hospital until you're properly on the mend—'

And so on, and so on. Really enjoying himself. At one point Peter had seriously begun to wonder whether God-Awful hadn't somehow found out about Peter's own virtuoso impressions of him, and had blushed scarlet with shame at the thought; he had felt his face glowing, as it was again now, just remembering that moment of horrible suspicion.

Oh hell, hell. Peter ran his hand again over the fur. It was, he thought resentfully, all Annie's fault. At the thought of her the inner trembling reached a sudden crescendo, and made him want to whimper out loud. It had all been her idea anyway.

'Honest it'd look really great. If it was really short.'

Of course he'd never taken it seriously. He hadn't planned it or even thought about it, he'd just ducked into this entirely unfamiliar place he'd never so much as looked at before, and sat down in front of the mirror and that smarmy adolescent, and demanded the works.

'Are you quite sure?'

'Absolutely!'

Rather a feminine thing to do really, Peter thought to himself as the trembling faded. The sort of thing he'd read women did anyway. Get chucked, get a new look. Wasn't it often the way the ex-partner had wanted you to look, as well?

Peter grinned to himself, looked up, and saw Joe hesitating in the doorway. He waved the paper, bracing himself for the inevitable double-take. It came.

'Interesting,' said Joe, approaching a few minutes later with his pint. There was a short pause, while he sat down and avoided looking at Peter's head. After a minute or so he made a sudden snorting noise, prelude to a giggling fit. Peter laughed as well, one hand over his eyes.

'Jesus,' said Joe at last.

'Yes,' said Peter, agreeing.

'What brought that on?'

Peter shrugged. 'Oh, I don't know. Felt like a change, I suppose. Split up with Annie.'

'Oh?'

'Yeah. Tuesday. Out of the blue. I mean, I know she got fed up now and then. But—' He shrugged again.

He looked awful, Joe noticed, face all white and scrawny. Or was that just the haircut?

'She gave me this ultimatum, I said no . . .'

The vagueness, Joe knew, would soon give way to detailed exposition. He managed not to sigh. I told her it wouldn't work, he reflected.

56

'Well, that's the point!' she'd cried. 'If he turns me down, I won't have lost anything, I'll know he was never mine to lose. It's not a ploy, you know. I really mean it.' So perhaps she really had.

'We went to this awful park near where she lives,' said Peter. 'It was just football pitches, hundreds of them, hardly any trees, just empty goal-posts. It was vile.'

They had walked along quite fast against the cold wind that swept across the cropped featureless grass, stopping finally beside a choked-up stream-bed full of nettles.

'. . . Then you just don't love me enough,' she'd said.

'No,' he had at last agreed. 'I suppose I just don't.'

Remembering this made Peter's eyes ache. He picked up his glass. How could he have said such a thing? To Annie?

Because it was true, he told himself, but all the same he saw his own tears dripping onto the sleeve of her black leather jacket as she held onto his arm.

I do love her, but not enough, it's something wrong with me, not with her . . .

No. He shook himself. That wouldn't do, scrub that out. That was soppy teenage rubbish. And he'd even said it before to Ghislaine, after that dreadful and as it turned out final weekend in Cornwall; he could remember the answering look she'd shot him even now.

'I know you'll find someone else, it won't take you long,' Annie had said. 'But you were really meant for me all the same. You'll never replace me, no one else will ever measure up, not really. This is all your fault. You are doing this, not me.'

Rehearsed, he told himself. But still it had frightened him.

'I feel a bit funny actually,' he said now.

'Here,' said Joe, pushing over his crisps.

'Ta.' Peter sniffed. 'Haven't eaten all day,' he said.

And rather pleased about it, thought Joe. Proves he's feeling something. What's he need proof for? Joe had never felt he needed it himself. But then judging by the way most

57

people carried on it was Peter who was the normal one. It was his usual conclusion, but still it was depressing.

'You look like a psychopath,' he said aloud.

'Yeah. I know. Tell you something else. I keep getting these looks. From other blokes.'

'What, you mean—'

Peter nodded. 'I hadn't realised. Had you? It's a sign, apparently.' Rob Tenislow, during the Finance Sub-Committee this afternoon: a definite. I hadn't known. He looks straight enough. But that sudden interested glance, an inflection of the eyes, a clear question:

Yes?

And the boy in the paper shop on the way here:

Yes?

Easy enough, of course, politely to signal No. But then again:

'There was a bunch of yobs outside the newsagent's giving me the eye as well.' Three of them, young, rather heavily built, almost fat, in clean blue jeans and brown leather jackets. Not the glad eye, far from it; he had felt them grow still as he passed them. It had been an effort, not walking any faster, not taking a quick look round as he turned the corner. Gay-bashers, presumably. Or anyone-who-asks-for-it-bashers.

'D'you think it looks aggressive?'

'It'll only last three weeks,' said Joe. 'Or thereabouts.'

Peter picked up his glass. Three weeks of being smiled at by men with earrings or beaten up by men with tattoos. Or both. And Annie would—

His stomach turned over with panic again, funny how he kept forgetting, no more Annie, that was all done with, she'd thrown him over.

'You're doing this, not me,' she had said, so proud of her lack of pride, that's what she was like, completely honest, oh Annie—

'You'll never replace me.' Suppose it was true? Look at old Joe after all.

'All those times I thought I'd touched your soul!' She'd been crying when she said that.

'You had, you did!'

What had he been playing at, trying to reassure her, saying it had all been real when hardly a minute before he'd been passionately arguing that it hadn't?

'All those times I thought I'd touched your soul!' Gasped out, between sobs, it kept coming back to him like a line from a song, and it still made him tremble. It was the sort of thing real emotion made you say, he had realised, and all his occasional efforts since to dismiss it as sickly and banal had only made him feel ashamed of himself, for trying to sneer at the truth in the name of good taste.

'You all right?'

Peter nodded. He blew his nose.

'Hey. There's a party tonight.'

'What party?'

'Friend of mine,' said Joe. 'From biotechnology.'

'What, beetles?'

'No. Yeast.'

There was a pause. 'Actually,' said Peter at last, 'I think I'd rather not. Not tonight, anyway.'

'Oh. Right-oh then.'

'You go.'

'Nah, I don't care, that's okay.' Joe sat back, slowly poking crisps into his mouth, thinking, twelve, so that's what, twenty years, twenty years he's never turned down a party before, not anyone's anywhere.

. . . just get beaten up anyway, Peter was thinking. Or frighten women. Must've been mad.

'D'you remember when we rode over to Golders Green that time?' said Joe. 'On our bikes? My mum hit me round the head when I got back.'

'Did she?' Peter grinned. 'You never said.'

Always making me go as well, thought Joe, without resentment. That one in St John's Wood—

'D'you remember that one in St John's Wood? When you

59

opened the wrong door, and locked us out into the back garden, pitch dark, bloody freezing—'

'It was you. You locked us out.'

'No. It was you. Wasn't it?'

Someone put the music on, pleasant, nothing special, and the polar-bear man strolled over to the bar, still fondly entwined. I'm safe here, thought Peter, watching him pass. Safe here from everything for the moment.

'Wasn't it?' he repeated. He smiled. 'Perhaps it was me, then.'

12

'SEE WHAT IT IS, IS THIS,' SAID ANNIE LOUDLY. 'YOU can't assume anything about them, they're not like ordinary nurses, you know, nice. Ordinary nurses, they might make mistakes, they might be dim as all get-out, but they're nearly always nice, and they're really upset at being before a tribunal; you have to be all gentle, sometimes they're practically in tears, they're so anxious. But not RMNs, oh no, no Mental Nurses, completely different kettle of fish, more like gaolers, they've got so much power, you see, over such weak people, and you can't help but think, that's why, that's why they're in this job, institutionalised power, and *no doubt*,' Annie sneered, so suddenly vehement that Marion jumped in her chair, 'no doubt there's lots of good ones, the majority for all I know, but the ones I meet are absolute bastards.'

Marion, throughout most of this, so longed to lie down that she could hardly keep still. Mere fidgeting made her lean across and empty the last of the wine into Annie's glass.

'Ta,' said Annie immediately, picking the glass up and taking another big swig. 'And this one today, God! Did I tell you it was me in charge?'

'Yes, you—'

'What a sod, what an absolute sod!'

Marion yawned helplessly. Her eyes itched and watered. It was nearly midnight. When it's twelve, she told herself, I'll just say it, Annie, please, I've just got to get some sleep—

'We should've got rid of him,' said Annie. 'I wanted him out.'

There was a pause, while Marion thought about this.

'What – you mean, given him the sack?' Marion felt suddenly very upset, but for the moment put this down to Annie's manner rather than her words.

'Absolutely,' said Annie. 'He's the Charge Nurse, right? And he's useless, there have been so many accidents, too many suicide attempts, three since he took over, and he's definitely shifting NHS patients over to this private clinic he's involved with – he's obviously getting some sort of rake-off – and then he's always off sick.'

'He can't help that, surely.'

'He's moonlighting, the bastard! Doing his time at the private place. Leaving his own ward up shit creek.'

'So you sacked him then, did you?' It was Marion's voice, at once hard in tone and slightly tremulous, that made her realise the cause of her own distress as she spoke.

She's been having me on, she thought miserably. Making out it was all form-filling and staring out of windows. To cheer me up. Because she knows all I'm working on at the moment is getting three hours' sleep in a row. Being tactful to poor Marion, well why should I care? I've never wanted her job, have I? Hospital administrator no thanks, she's welcome to it—

All the same the sense of being left behind, seedily unemployable, while Annie rose higher and higher, carried up now not only by her own efforts, but by smooth career-structure machinery, in which growing older also meant seniority and distinction, was almost overwhelming; Marion felt quite shaken, and got up rather jerkily to put the kettle on.

'Well, no, actually,' said Annie, turning round. 'I mean I still had to confer,' she added bitterly. 'I had to give him a First Written Warning. Not even a slapped wrist really. It'll be off his record in a year.'

And of course all this is really about Peter, thought Marion, shaking the match out. She looked over at Annie, remembering the pang she had felt on first seeing her that evening on the doorstep clutching her bottle of wine: she'd looked so drawn. Making herself ill over some bloke, thought Marion, almost herself again. She felt rather nostalgic; post-natally it was hard to take all that stuff quite seriously .

'I'll make some tea, and then I've just got to get to bed, okay.' she said gently.

'Oh God, I'm sorry, keeping you up like this, look, I'll go now, I've got my bike—'

'Don't be daft, you're drunk. You stay here.'

'Oh. All right then.'

'The sofa's not bad actually – I'll just get some blankets, just a sec—'

Annie sat back happily, for the thought of her own empty flat and, worse, empty bed, had nagged at her all evening, for reasons she had, she realised, completely avoided going into, though Marion was the obvious person to discuss them with, and she'd come over tonight on purpose, to do so; what had gone wrong?

'Do you remember Danny Moran,' she asked, as Marion trudged back in with the bedding, 'that I was so in love with when I was sixteen?'

'Just about. Why? Did you want tea?'

'Yes, please. I really fancied him, I mean, he only had to touch me—' and I got that entirely localised sensation, she had imagined herself saying; can't though. That time saying goodbye to him at the railway station, I couldn't wait for him to get on the train and go, because that coarse throbbing between my legs was so hateful to me.

Yes, that's what I can't say, not even to Marion, though it's probably just the same for her. I mean was.

'And I went to bed with his brother, because I liked him, I liked the look of him and I could talk to him' without any physical sensations 'and I thought that was fancying him. Whereas I couldn't stand the way Danny made me feel, I didn't know what it was, it was frightening.'

'I remember now,' said Marion, sitting down with the tea. 'I remember him coming round once nearly in tears, wasn't he at the front door—?'

'While I got out at the back with Philip, yes,' said Annie, noticing again how jolly and Chaucerian this episode looked from some angles, and how miserable and shaming it had felt at the time. Because I was fucking the wrong one, she thought. I was fucking the one I could talk about Dostoevsky with.

'What brought this on, anyway?'

'What, Danny? Oh, I don't know. Nothing,' said Annie. She inspected her tea, it looked greasy somehow. Hungover already, she thought, sipping it all the same. Still I won't be on my own, she remembered. And this was like one in the eye for him, a little victory; for almost her first thought, as the door closed behind him had been of herself, alone in her bed that night, succumbing to fear.

But fear of what? Not of him, not really. Annie closed her eyes. There was the tribunal, herself dark and neat behind the desk, flanked by juniors and her boss just sitting in and the trade union official, all of them facing the nurse in question. She could see it quite clearly, as if it were a picture in a book about management, everyone would look all right in an illustration. Why had it all felt so different? Perhaps it was a matter of scale, she thought, you could see why law courts went in for high ceilings and elevated benches and judges hiding under wigs.

But in that ordinary room, with ordinary blond modern furniture and a potted plant, he could look right into her eyes. And everything about him, his unstudied relaxed

64

position in his chair, his open-necked shirt and trainers, his grin for the union man, had let her know exactly what he thought about the proceedings, with an extra little gleam just for her, because she was young and a woman.

And she'd known even beforehand that the case was a non-starter, the Filipino ward-maid who'd seen him bashing Jim Burnside against a filing cabinet had hopped it back to the Philippines, and Julia Melchior had backed down at the last minute: there was almost nothing to go on. As he no doubt already knew.

'Mr Paulford—'

'Miss Grey.'

Not only slightly aggressive, that instant come-back use of her name, but very faintly teasing, a promise of patient masculine indulgence whilst he was here, a grown-up guest in her Wendy house: a tone he would never have used to any man. She had not expected deliberate insult, not so soon anyway; it took her a second or so to rally.

Look, to a man he'd've used something else.

He did it on purpose, don't rise to it.

Watch out.

'Mr Paulford,' pause. Look at me, yes, what insult? I didn't notice, see? 'What is the crash call for your ward?'

Ahah! Silent. Got you, don't change face, too high-up for triumph, stay blank. Got you got you.

'Mr Paulford? In an emergency?'

Shaking his head, trying to look bemused. No, no use looking at the trade union man, he won't know.

'I'm sorry, I can't remember.'

Bluff-but-honest.

'You are in charge of the ward. Don't you think you should know the crash call?'

'Yes of course, but—'

'It's 911, Mr Paulford, perhaps you should make a note of it?'

But that had been the high point really, it had been all downhill after that.

'. . . just recommended a place I know, that's all. They were being discharged, too early in my opinion, but we hadn't got the beds. They asked me, their relations asked me, I told them, that's all . . .'

'. . . well yes, I did a shift there, but just the once, I'd double-booked myself, my mistake, it won't happen again. But you show me a nurse who's never done an extra shift here and there, we can hardly get by without it on NHS pay.'

His faint extra emphasis towards the end of this asked her, lightly, how much she earned herself, in her clean safe office, told her, indulgently, that whilst in it, in her clean safe Wendy house, she did nothing, nothing worth doing, nothing real at all.

Whereas, thought Annie at him now, her hands warm round her teacup, you yourself are proof otherwise. This is my job: to eliminate the brutal, the corrupt, the incompetent, and you are all three, I know it.

Exciting, to feel this, no, more, intoxicating; I hardly needed the wine, thought Annie. But I wanted to tell Marion, I thought that I would.

Odd how much the First Written Warning had upset him. It had enraged him, his voice had actually trembled.

'Well I have every intention of lodging an appeal!' Silly git, Annie had thought in surprise. All that John Waynery and then whimpering over a Warning, it was pathetic.

'That's up to you of course.' Very dismissive. 'I think that's everything for now.'

He'd stood up, his hands on the chair-back, rather slender delicate hands, she had noticed, wished them all a sarcastic good morning, glanced deliberately at her, and taken himself off, banging the door behind him.

'Well!' One of the juniors, exclaiming, close to laughter; his emotion had embarrassed them all.

Annie had bent over her desk, briskly shuffling papers together to hide her flaming face. No one had ever looked at her like that before. She was used to anger, the usual office explosions, tempers barely under control, even the odd furious bollocking given or received; but no one else in all her adult life had so clearly wanted to do her physical harm. Not only that; there had been another message along with the simple menace.

He would have whispered it, the message, she thought, stood close and whispered it to her, if he could.

'I'd fuck you first.'

She had felt it knock into her, her whole body had instantly flared with outrage and shock, so that her hands trembled, sorting her papers; and all the time, at the same time—

You have to call it sexual response, Annie told herself, reasonably, now. That immediate localised throb.

But look. No one knows but you. He certainly doesn't. Didn't. He just gave you a nasty look and made off.

'I'd fuck you first.'

Presumably a normal physiological response to threat, thought Annie; hadn't she read somewhere of women responding in rape?

'Oh God!' she said aloud, 'Marion, you know when—' But Marion, her head rolled to one side, her hands still clasped round her empty cup, was clearly asleep. 'Marion?'

Annie sighed. It had been part of the fear, she thought, remembering Danny Moran at the railway station: the idea that the man somehow knew of your sensations, that he could sneer at you for helplessly responding, responding all over him, disgusting, like being sick on his shoes—

This is sexual disgust, thought Annie, unconsciously crossing her legs and folding her arms, he has made me remember sexual disgust, he has made me feel it, for him; and if sexual disgust feels more or less indistinguishable from sexual desire that's nothing to be ashamed of, it's just another huge design fault on a flaming great listful and absolutely nothing to do with me.

But I am ashamed.

She thought again of the picture they had made, the

67

perfect textbook illustration of a minor industrial tribunal. In all outward ways nothing much had happened, an incompetent employee had been criticised, had defended himself, had been officially rebuked. It was perplexing; it all looked fine on paper, it would all look perfectly ordinary in the report, no one had in truth contemptuously told her she was a footling overpaid bureaucrat or given way to brutish rage and threatened to violate and murder her; it was simply ridiculous to go on trembling and moping as if someone really had.

Nor was it appropriate, either, to try instead to fight back, to make herself feverishly restless all over from picturing the next time, even though there was of course going to be a next time – he was her job, he was brutal, corrupt, and incompetent.

I'll get him next time, she had told herself, riding over to Marion's, and the menacing power of the phrase had made her accelerate through a red light.

'I'll get you next time, you little shit!'

Not appropriate; undignified; it still meant thinking about him all the time and since it didn't come quite naturally anyway keeping it going was just as exhausting, after a while, as trembling and moping.

Peter. I could have told him. He'd've been so interested. Prurient sod, thought Annie, almost smiling. I could've told him, he'd've been interested and sympathetic and angry for me and just excited enough and amused. He'd've made me laugh about it. And taken the taste away, by—

No. Don't think about that. That won't do at all. Don't be so feeble, thought Annie, sitting up and straightening herself out on the sofa. Now. Wake her up. Get organised. God knows what time it is.

'Marion. Marion, sorry, hallo—'

'Hallo,' said Marion. Danny Moran, still seventeen, had wheeled his bicycle into her front room and smiled at her as sweetly as a child. 'She's in the back,' said Marion, and smiled at him in her sleep.

13

IT WAS LOADING THE CAR THAT HELD THEM UP. Travel cot, foam mattress, sheet, spare sheet, sheepskin, cot-duvet, nappies, babywipes, little box of scented plastic bags for the dirty nappies ('Yes, yes, I know,' Marion had cut in before Benny had a chance to start complaining, 'but they haven't got any children, have they, they've got no idea'), carrying-sling, pushchair with raincover, highchair, padded seat for highchair, wellington boots, snowsuit, rainsuit, huge plastic bag full of clothes, toys for the bath, a plastic train set, a dozen little bottles of baby food and exotic fruit juices, an electric blender and several teats and dummies swimming about in a small tupperware box of sterilising fluid.

'I can't bloody see out!'

'Just put it beside him then, he can have that one beside him and this one can go under his feet, look, it squashes right down—'

'We can't need half this stuff, it's only a weekend.'

'We'll only need it if we don't take it,' said Marion, reasonably, she thought. She rolled the sheepskin into a fat sausage shape and forced it behind the baby-seat.

'There. Satisfied?'

'Where are you putting your stuff, then?'

'I'm not taking much.'

'What are you going to wear, then, tomorrow night?'

'What d'you mean?'

'Well, you might feel a bit out of it, you know, if everyone else is all done up.'

'What everyone else? I thought it was just us.'

'They might have other people round. You know, for supper. They're always having people round.'

'I haven't got anything.'

'Yes you have. That blue one, that's nice; that'd be all right.'

'It's ancient. It makes me look fat.'

'No it doesn't. I like it anyway, I've always liked that one.'

Marion was silent. A whole new set of things to worry about had presented themselves. The blue dress would need the right shoes, the ones with the bows in front, she'd seen one of them mysteriously all by itself on the bathroom floor wasn't it last week? But not, surely, today, so where could it have got to now, and where might the other one be? And new tights, and the petticoat for the dress, hadn't come across that for months, and make-up, and earrings, and something to tie back her hair with . . .

'Oh Lord.' She had not, she realised, given any of these essentials a moment's thought, had simply stuffed her toothbrush and some clean underwear into her handbag; further proof, if any were needed, of how completely Lewis had supplanted her as the object of her own existence. Is that right? she wondered, is it normal? Is it good for him or will it squash him flat somehow?

'You all right?'

'What? Yes, I'm fine, I'd just sort of forgotten I was going too.'

'We haven't been away for ages.'

'No,' said Marion shortly, and went back into the house, where Lewis lay propped in his playpen watching *Sesame Street*. She crept past him unnoticed and ran upstairs. In the bedroom she took her blue dress out and held it up to the light. There was a smear of something on one shoulder, she noticed; Lewis must've burped. She scrubbed the mark against itself, and it powdered: dried milk: indelible.

'Oh no!' And nothing else would do, not stuck at nine and a half stone like this. Apart from the maternity stuff everything she owned was pre-pregnant, chosen to show off slenderness; even the loose-fitting things looked all wrong now, not floaty and elegant any more but filled in solid. And she had so far been unable to bring herself to buy anything new, not simply because spending money on the still-unfamiliar buxom frump in the mirror would mean accepting her as permanent, or at the very least long term, but also because it would mean a whole new approach to clothes, choosing things not for emphasis any more but for disguise.

I just can't face it, thought Marion; meaning her sensation of joining a vast unlovely company, the camp of boring fatties, met at school and at work and in the women's magazines, the ones who were always on diets and knew their own thigh measurements and the calorific value of absolutely everything off by heart, the ones who carefully ate Ryvita spread with cottage cheese at lunchtime, or sipped at frothy milkshakes full of bulk-producing cellulose and mineral supplements, and who never seemed to lose an inch or a pound or two for more than five minutes; after a lifetime's casual, unthinking (even cruel, it seemed to her now) slenderness, she had joined the company of fatties for ever perhaps, and now, helplessly weighty and protuberant, she must go away for a glamorous weekend in the country with nothing to wear but a tired old dress flecked with vomit.

'Ooooh!' wailed Marion, and she lay back on the unmade bed, and pulled the dress over her face, and lay still for a moment, quite overcome.

'What's up? Marion? Are you all right?'

71

Marion sat up, and pulled the dress off her head. She gave a long trembling sigh.

'I don't see how I can go,' she said.

'What?'

'Look.'

'What at?'

'This. There, look!'

'Oh. Well. Won't notice. Couldn't you wash it, just that bit?'

Marion shook her head dismally. She felt too tired to move.

'I'll do it. Give it to me, I'll do it, it'll dry on the way down.' Benny sat down beside her on the bed. 'It won't show, honest.'

'It's not just that. I'm so, I'm so fat, and, horrible, oh—'

'You're huge,' said Benny into her hair. 'You're vast, you're a whopper, I don't know how you get through doors.'

She had to smile.

'Shall I do it then?' He gave the dress a little tug.

'No, no. It's okay, I'll do it.' Rather abruptly Marion slid out from beneath his arm. It was a bit much frankly, she told herself, as she ran the cold tap in the bathroom. It's a bit much to come strolling in all supportive after months and months of being a wet rag and disappearing whenever he feels like it. Looking at me like that. What's he expect?

Benny lay back on the bed and stared up at the ceiling. He remembered the last time they had gone away for the weekend, shortly before Lewis's birth. He had thought of it fairly frequently ever since, for it was also the last time he and Marion had been lovers. She'd hidden under the bedclothes, wanted to keep her nightie on. It was true she'd got absolutely enormous, not just the swollen stomach anyone would expect, but everywhere, huge tense bosoms, thighs all over the place, even her arms were getting fat towards the end; but he hadn't minded, not really, not anything like as much as she had; in fact he'd liked the bosoms very much, and she had liked him to touch them, then, had got him to massage them, very gently, with olive oil, they had slid beneath his fingers, magnificent resilient fruit, could you sort of knead them? she'd said, no, a bit harder, that's lovely, oh that's nice—

'You could have straightened up a bit in here.' Marion in the doorway, sharpish. The dress hung limply from her hand.

Benny sat up. 'Has it come off?'

'It says Dry Clean Only. I suppose it'll be all right. It'll have to be, that's all.'

Benny got up, and tugged without conviction at the duvet, not that it was his, he reflected, how come it's me always gets the Z-bed? You'd think we could swop now and then.

'No, not like that, like this,' said Marion smartly.

14

RUSSELL HAD LARGELY STOPPED THINKING ABOUT that Miss Grey. For a few days he had thought of little else, and felt himself to be implacable. One or two interesting ideas had come to him, quite small prankish things really, more to discomfit and annoy her than terrorise: bombarding her with junk mail trial offers, for instance, or booking her a series of insurance salesmen and double-glazing experts.

But all this sort of thing hinged on knowing her address, and faced with discovering this his implacability tended to go off the boil. To be spotted trying to follow her home would be disastrous; insinuating himself into her office impossible, given the security at reception; arranging to have her mugged pleasant to consider but again fraught with risk, involving, as of course it would, some intrinsically untrustworthy third party.

It was easier, therefore, to give up being implacable, and turn to being easy-going instead, the sort of guy who shrugged his shoulders at malice. But by the second of his next two days off he found himself very much bothered by the thought of what he would now be so busily up to had he stayed vengeful: planning, tracking her down, making notes of her movements, marking down her friends and relations: the usual game overpoweringly transformed.

'Just a little game,' Russell told himself that afternoon as he got his jacket on and picked up his keys. Following some silly woman and giving her a little fright, that was the game of If I Were A Maniac. This one was If I Were A Vengeful Maniac. After all, he thought, I'm not going to do anything. I'm just going to hang about seeing what it would feel like if I were.

He set off in high spirits, and reached her office building still buoyant, his heart actually pounding. He walked up the street and down again, feeling himself to be a sinister presence, imagining the music that would accompany him if he were in a film. Which was all very well for five minutes or so, but the day had turned very cold. The damp wind made his eyes water.

Of course in a film there was always a café opposite, with big useful windows, so that the trailing detective or psychopath could sit scanning the doors in comfort. Whereas here there wasn't so much as a bus-stop to lean against. He walked up and down again, beginning to shiver – should've put another jumper on, I'll catch pneumonia, this is ridiculous, this is a complete waste of time – when Annie opened the big swing doors and stood for a moment not twenty feet away on the steps, putting big leather gloves on. She was wearing peculiar bulky trousers, and carrying a large red crash helmet.

A crash helmet?

Shit, said Russell under his breath, resisting the impulse to flatten himself against the nearest wall. Instead he turned his back, counted to three, and turned round again in time to see her making off in the other direction, swinging the crash helmet in one hand. Russell walked quickly after her, reaching a hand inside his jacket as he did so, pulling out a biro with numb, shaking fingers. Close enough to hear the sound the padded nylon trousers made, swishing together as she walked, he carried on past her when, just round the corner, she stopped by a row of parked motorbikes.

Russell bent, pretending to re-tie the laces on his trainers while she started up the engine, straightening just in time to read the number plate as she moved out into the road, then turning away quickly because of her wing mirror, nice touch that, he told himself. He wrote the number down on the inside cover of his cheque book, and then, judging it safe, looked up again. Yes, there she was. Prissy little Honda, just what you'd expect. Nipping through the traffic, unreachable

So what would I do, if I were a vengeful maniac? Russell walked on until he came to a Wimpy bar, and went inside to thaw out. Nobble her bike. Do something to the brakes or the steering. Or let the tyres down so she had to take the tube. Could I follow her on the tube?

The beat of excitement suddenly made him tremble. Borrow Barney's motorbike, of course. She'd never spot me in a crash helmet. Just another biker, roaring along behind, the obvious solution. Only playing, of course.

I know where you live. That was what you said to people, when you wanted to frighten them. Soon. I'll know where she lives.

He felt warm all over now. He looked down at his own thighs spread on the plastic bench. They seemed tense with vitality. For a moment he was aware of his entire self, within his clothes but quite apart from them, as if he were sitting there wearing only his own glorious muscles.

The moment passed as abruptly as it had arrived, and he was himself again, sipping a coffee, and already sceptical. That was Jekyll and Hyde, he thought, that was that bloke who used to go bright green and burst all his shirt buttons, that was just me remembering all sorts of bits and pieces: nothing real.

He paid for the coffee, eleven shillings, who'd've believed it, eleven bob for a cup of coffee! and set off for home, to telephone Barney.

15

MRS DOWNELY LIVED JUST ROUND THE CORNER, AS she had said. So that was reassuring; if she turns out weird I can always nip back to the pub, thought Janet.

'They were service flats originally,' said Mrs Downely, inserting various keys, 'with a doorman and a restaurant on the ground floor; one could order meals and have them sent up on a dumb-waiter. Though actually,' – the great door swung open – 'it was pretty awful food really, you're much better off with something from Marks and Spencers and a microwave oven. Absurd, this idea that people ever used to cook their own dinners. Look at Dickens, they're always sending out for things, entire meals, all even Little Dorrit does is heat something up in a pan, d'you read Dickens?'

'No.'

'Given her dinner at work, you see, and instead of eating it herself she smuggles it out of the house God knows how, it's some sort of stew, I believe, and takes it back for her disgusting old father in prison, and her admirer happens to call while she's warming it up over the open fire, and I of course thought straight away, I mean for God's sake, it's this meaty stew, has she got a non-stick pan or something, I couldn't help but see the whole scene played out against this frightful smell of burning fat and poor Little Dorrit wordlessly struggling in a corner, scraping this mess about, smoke everywhere, everyone pretending nothing was happening—' Mrs Downely became quite helpless with laughter, and leant up against the wall, wiping her eyes.

'Because of course,' she went on, yanking the door open at the third floor, 'and I've never read this anywhere, though I'm sure it must have occurred to someone else, the most interesting thing about books, no, not the most interesting of course but *one* of the most interesting things, is that while you're reading them you set the scene. And you usually don't notice, unless you stop reading and make a conscious effort to note the surroundings you have conjured up. Have you ever done that?'

'No.'

'*Wuthering Heights* I first noticed it in, when I was quite a child, do come in. I simply adored *Wuthering Heights*, I used to sit reading it over and over again until I knew great chunks of it off by heart, and after a while I realised that I had made the house, you know, Wuthering Heights itself, in the image of the church we all used to go to, a very ordinary modern chapel-of-ease it was, perfectly suburban, anyway there was the ghost of Catherine Earnshaw creeping about outside the vestry, there was Heathcliff howling out of the window by the parish war memorial; once I'd noticed it I somehow couldn't take the book seriously anymore. It was rather a loss really. And after that I found I was doing it all the time: putting scenes in, well, simply the wrong place usually; I have to make an effort not to look too closely, as it were, at the edges of my own imagination, in case it turns out to be Euston station that Anna Karenina is lurking about in, or quite often the Food Hall at Harrods, would you like tea, dear, or something to drink? I've got nearly everything.'

'Tea would be nice.'

The front room was large and warm, and full of things

that Janet immediately wanted a closer look at, little china figures in a cabinet, three tiny silver boxes on a table by the armchair, a sleek wooden case of photographs, curious double photographs, Janet saw, with one already set into some sort of viewing glass.

How young she looks, such a little thing, and so sullen, marvelled Mrs Downely. She would have liked to touch Janet's cheek. It was years, she thought, since anyone's appearance had made her wish for their company.

'Take a look,' she said.

Janet picked the thing up, and held it to her eyes, and after a moment saw that through it the two images combined. 'Oh, I had one of these, when I was a kid. Scenes from *Bambi*, it was.'

'Well, that's the Great Gardens of Europe, extraordinarily boring but the clothes are rather nice, I'll just put the kettle on, excuse me—'

Janet concentrated, and entered the picture, like Alice. Through it she was standing on a path in a faded black-and-white land, being looked at herself by two rather squat Victorian ladies holding parasols.

'Odd, isn't it,' said Mrs Downely from the doorway, 'the difference it makes? I mean that they're not smiling. If they were smiling you would think, how lovely, what a beautiful garden, don't you think? Two people enjoying a sunny morning in the Boboli gardens, captured forever, that sort of thing. Of course they couldn't smile even if they'd wanted to, not for ten minutes at a time. But if they *were* smiling they would be the point of the picture and they would incidentally show up the loveliness of the garden. As it is they are merely part of a composition, and so it is a document of place, not time, and therefore pretty dull. Apart from their clothes, I think the one on the right looks dreadfully like Toad of Toad Hall in his washer-woman phase, don't you? Such a fallacy, the idea that long skirts and corsets and so on were flattering to everyone, short fat women must have looked completely spherical and, God knows, big fat women must have looked simply grotesquely enormous, walking bedsteads, now I really am off—'

Janet, left alone, lowered the viewing glass and eyed herself in the large mirror over the fireplace. It was hardly the first time she had gone home with someone whose behaviour and conversation were completely mystifying, but then quite a few of the other occasions had led to one thing or another, more than once pretty peculiar. She sighed uneasily, and took up another double photograph.

In the kitchen Mrs Downely stood still for a moment, considering tactics. *Upstairs, Downstairs* opulence, she thought, was probably the right note to go for. But not too intimidatingly formal. She laid the tray with an embroidered cloth, pretty but mismatching teacups, her pink lustre milk jug, and two slices of fruit cake. And do try to relax, she told herself reasonably. Stop trying to make her smile. Because she won't. Or quite possibly can't.

She is like one of those shop assistants, thought Mrs Downely as the kettle boiled, who make no apology when whatever it is you've just asked for is no longer in stock, who answer flatly, with a shrug, disclaiming all responsibility, no doubt with logic on their side. Though I suspect some absurd notion of integrity at work there as well, some plain refusal to simper for the upper classes. No smile, no apology, the uneasy menial's response.

'Where have you got to?'

'Versailles.'

No brightening at the sight of the tea-tray, noted Mrs Downely, no move politely indicative of the impulse to help put the thing down somewhere; just standing there, with her hands by her sides, positively surly, poor thing, thought Mrs Downely: it is a refusal to risk acting, it is a combination of integrity and fear, and therefore quite paralysing.

'Do sit down. And carry on with the Great Gardens if you like. I mean, don't try to sit there in silent appreciation, it's really much better to let it become familiar without

your being too aware of it, background music sort of thing.'
She picked up the first record. 'You've really never heard it
before? No? What have you been doing?'

A quick grin there, lovely.

'Milk and sugar?'

'Just milk.' The fanfare sounded like an air-raid siren.
Janet jumped.

'Cake?'

The men weighed in, harsh and booming.

*Thus spake Isaiah: thy sons that thou shalt beget, they
shall be taken away, and be eunuchs in the palace of the
king of Babylon. Howl ye, howl ye therefore; for the day of
the Lord is at hand.*

'Smashing stuff,' said Mrs Downely, swallowing hard
and lifting the needle for a moment. 'That repetition of
"howl" somehow completely removes any suggestion of the
comic, I mean, on its own, someone telling you to howl,
well, it would sound rather surprising and possibly a bit
ridiculous, don't you think, but repeated, he's saying,
Isaiah is saying, yes, this is what I mean, give yourself over
completely to despair, Howl ye, howl ye therefore, and of
course the men just love it, *maestoso*, I mean our choir, all
those perfectly nice solicitors and geography teachers, I
don't suppose they get the chance to be majestic and
terrifying every day, do you? I'm afraid we're much more
droopy, here we go:'

*By the waters of Babylon, there we sat down: yea, we
wept, and hanged our harps upon the willows—*

'You see? The altos actually being the waters there, as
well as the tears flowing. How did you ever make sense of
it, without having heard it first?'

'I didn't,' said Janet, 'mostly.'

'Don't listen to any more then. We will let it carry on,
but pay no attention to it. The trouble with this sort of
music, actually most sort of music as far as I'm concerned,
is that you can only really enjoy it if you know it already,
which of course leads to obvious difficulties with anything

new. You see how different that makes it from, say, a thriller at the pictures? You only need to see the thriller once, in fact you *can* only see it once. With the full excitement, I mean. Whereas with music you have to as it were know the plot already, you have to be on the edge of your seat waiting for the glorious or swoony bits. And it works best of all if it's something you have absolutely no memory of not knowing, you know, the "Hallelujah Chorus", something like that, put on the *Messiah* and all sorts of completely unmusical people flock to hear it, because it is so entirely familiar to them that even they can hear it properly, and they know they can sit through the boring bits, the interminable bass soloing and what not, because they know what's coming afterwards, in fact they enjoy the good bits all the more, having paid for them by having to keep still and fully awake while the Nations So Furiously Rage Together. Which does go on rather.'

'But.'

'Yes?'

'I don't think it's just that. I mean, most classical music. If I try to listen to it.'

'Yes?'

'Well, it sounds sad. Sort of, depressing.' Janet struggled; this was not quite what she had meant, but she was unable to see the difference clearly enough to correct herself.

'You mean, the sensation it evokes feels like sadness.'

'Do I?'

'Feels like yearning and loss?'

'Well. I'd rather see the thriller any day.'

'So would I. The trouble with trying to compare popular culture with art is that it leads you into all sorts of ludicrous fantasies, for instance, there you are shipwrecked on your desert island, now which would be of more use to you in your frightful isolation, a portable video machine showing *Casablanca* or a record player full of *Così fan tutte*? Art gets better, the more you know it; I dare say half a dozen

82

goes of *Casablanca* would be all that flesh and blood could stand, don't you?'

'Well—'

'And the sadness you describe is at least partly due to the uses we have put music to, in films and adverts and so on, it is the images that have been assigned to the music that you are remembering. Show a bit of beautiful unspoilt countryside, for example, tack on the right piece of Elgar, and the music is suddenly a hymn to loss, the sound of loss, not the celebration it probably started out as; use any music as accompaniment and it simply takes on the image supplied to it. Like material taking up a dye.'

There was a pause.

'There,' said Mrs Downely, 'the record's stopped and neither of us noticed, which is all to the good. Why don't you borrow it? Do the washing up to it. That's the best way, absorb it without knowing like the "Hallelujah Chorus", here you are.'

'Oh, I can't—'

'No, no. Quite all right. Bring it back on Tuesday, I'll give you the next bit.'

'I meant thank you, but I haven't got a record player.'

'Oh, I see. Well, I could tape it for you, I'd be glad to—'

'I haven't got a tape deck. Sorry.'

'Really? What do you—'

'I used to. I sort of—' Left everything behind, thought Janet, remembering all the various places she had abandoned things in, not just records and other hard-to-carry items like duvets and bookcases, but smaller stuff, pop-up toasters and cutlery, a particular pale-blue butter dish, I'm always having to buy things to take eggs out of frying pans with, I've always ended up leaving in a hurry, that's what it is.

'I sort of lose things. Leave them behind.'

'Really. How . . . careless.' Mrs Downely smiled.

'I came back from America once,' said Janet, 'after three years, with just my handbag. It felt great.'

'Did it? Why?'

'Well. I expected to feel miserable. I did most of the time, I'd just, you know, left someone, but every time I remembered I didn't own anything, not a thing, I sort of wanted to laugh, it cheered me up really.'

'Yes. I can see that it might.'

Janet stood up. 'I'd better be going now.'

'Um, I'll call you a cab, shall I?'

'No thanks. I'll get the tube, it's all right.'

'No it's not. Not really.'

'I'll be all right,' said Janet indifferently. 'Thanks for the tea.'

'Thank you for coming.' I don't get many visitors nowadays, thought Mrs Downely clearly, and was then only just able to stop herself from saying so out loud. Where on earth had that come from? she wondered as they reached the lift. 'See you next Tuesday.'

'Expect so. Good night.'

Any number of books and films, probably. It was the sort of thing people often made old ladies say, in order to show what a frightful business visiting the elderly generally was. So watch your lip, thought Mrs Downely to herself, sitting down rather gingerly, for getting tired always made her leg hurt more.

Not a single personal question, she noticed, looking back on her evening, which on the whole, she thought, had been rather a success, odd but interesting. She sat still for some time, trying to understand what it was about Janet that so attracted her, apart of course from the childlike curve of her cheek, wondering at last whether there was not some suggestion of darkness about her, unusual but still faintly familiar.

Ah, could that be it? Yes it could, yes, got it. It was a literary darkness, thought Mrs Downely, it was that same dank wintriness which tended to afflict the heroines of a certain type of early-Victorian novel. Alcott, say: hers were a glum hard-working black-and-white bunch, fevered all the time with a sexual energy which could find no natural outlet. Or Charlotte Brontë, look at Whatshername in *Villette*, head-down in a real fog of personal darkness, you could almost feel those long heavy skirts dragging at her ankles.

No wonder I went on and on about novels the poor girl had obviously never so much as looked at, and all that stuff about corsets and bedsteads – Mrs Downely laughed out loud. Extraordinary, she thought, to trace the origin of what had felt like a completely random set of little jokes; some part of me evidently spotted the dank Victorian heroine straight away.

And if you are seeing her as a heroine you had better watch out, thought Mrs Downely, teasing herself a little, for she felt herself to be far too old to be in any real danger from anything, anything at all, she remembered. Strange, this complete cessation of personal fear, strange but delightful, a source of almost bubbling power and energy.

'What's it matter to me if I do get mugged or run over or blown up by the IRA, I've had my life, don't you ever think that?' she had asked over bridge only the previous afternoon, and, one or two murmurs about grandchildren and great-grandchildren apart, everyone there had had to agree, some gleefully, some sighingly of course, but then poor dreary Pauline always had been one of life's sighers anyway.

Alcott rather than Brontë; less intelligence, more bursting repression. Mrs Downely yawned, and presently set off for bed.

Janet walked fast, striding along in her big black boots. She did not quite know whether to be disappointed or not. True, there had been some talk of the kind she had half hoped for, but then again also something unmistakable in

Mrs Downely's eyes as she'd come bustling in with her tea-tray. Well, I suppose lesbians have to grow old same as anyone else, thought Janet, but all the same she felt rather cheated. Oh, it's that, is it? she had asked herself, as Mrs Downely came in, just that again, that muddying things up again. Tea with an old lady, you surely had a right to expect clarity there.

It was the clarity of the Teddy Bear Postman that Janet was almost thinking about, or of the Teddy Bear Gardener, the old ladies he worked for brought him biscuits and lemonade, with no chance of anything perverse winking out of their kindly old eyes as they bent over him.

It's just like me, it's typical of me, thought Janet with disgust, far more disgust than she felt towards Mrs Downely herself. It was her own fault, she felt, the muddiness. She thought of her tidy, empty flat with longing, and without curiosity, and thus with no risk of noticing that it was not the tidy self-sufficiency of the Teddy Bear workers that so beguiled her, but their sexlessness.

She reached the station, and began to relax. Hope that sodding cat's held off, she'd had to mop the hallway twice while Marion had been away. Still she was back now, judging by the million or so plastic bags lining the passage that morning. Lovely and quiet, the weekend had been, without all that constant bickering and door-slamming and infant howling drifting up the stairs.

On the other hand it was pleasant to feel there was someone in, especially someone you didn't have to talk to. Janet hurried along the dark street, almost eagerly, nearly home, but at the front gate stopped short. It had happened again, then. Kids, presumably. But why just this dustbin, and not next door's? It was all over the tiny front yard where someone had parked their Honda, there was even something wet and nasty-looking on its seat, horrible, wonder if Marion knows?

Suppose I'd better tell her, thought Janet, no, I'll leave

it till morning, she's not going to want to do anything about it now anyway. Yuk.

She opened the door, to be met by a strong smell of Dettol.

16

THE FIRST HALF HOUR WAS PAR FOR THE COURSE:
when, after about three minutes, Lewis's high-pitched
roaring screams became quite unendurable, Marion had
climbed through into the back seat, squeezed herself almost
into a sitting position there, unstrapped him, and fed him,
which had immediately calmed him down, but, just outside
Notting Hill Gate, at a price. Though she had efficiently
packed a separate bag of emergency clothes, Marion could
not, she soon realised, identify it amongst all the others,
and had to burrow around, difficult when she was sitting
on two or three of them and still holding on to Lewis, who,
upset perhaps by his mother's fierce scrabblings, began
bawling again, and struggled wildly when she had finally
come up with a fresh babygro, kicking his little chicken
legs about in the complicated trouser-part so that she kept
doing the poppers up wrong. Then, just as she was ladling
him back into his seat, he had suddenly, forcibly filled his
nappy, overwhelming it, thought Marion resignedly; no
nappy on earth could have been expected to cope, you'd
think he was going for some sort of record.

'We'll have to stop!'

'We're on the motorway for Christ's sake!'

Still, the long struggle had worn him out and after about

ten minutes of being clapped to and sung Postman Pat his eyelids had drooped, and his small bald head had fallen sideways. Marion went on humming loudly for another five minutes, for giving up too soon had, in the past, proved disastrous; after that she counted twenty-five regular breaths, and felt it was safe to assume that he was, almost certainly, asleep. Very slowly, the plastic bags heaving and crackling alarmingly beneath her, she inched her way forwards, and clambered as noiselessly as possible into the front again, hardly daring to breathe.

There was a silence. At length Benny risked a whisper. 'Has he gone?'

Marion peeped backwards. Several times, on other trips, she had taken a quick look back and Lewis had seemed to sense her glance in his sleep and snapped his eyes open, and she had had to start the whole process again, three more goes of Postman Pat, clapping, humming, counting. But this time all was well.

'I think so.'

'Christ for that.' They smiled at one another. Marion stretched in her seat, luxuriously. A good hour, she thought happily, he'd be away for at least an hour, and there was absolutely nothing she could do, or ought to be doing, other than sitting here comfortably looking out of the window, or closing her eyes. Lovely, a holiday.

'He's thinking of going on tour again,' said Benny eventually.

'Who is? What?'

'Mel is.' Benny kept his eyes on the road. 'That's partly why he asked us down.'

'What, he wants you to go?'

Benny nodded, darting a look at her. He will be excited if I am, thought Marion, and blasé if I am. He is waiting to find out what to feel.

Well, which would be most useful? A tour would mean lots of practice, in his own flat of course, and then the off, and so he'd be out of her hair for at least two or three months; and he'd certainly be cheerful at first, having something to do for a change, and of course there'd be money, eventually. Presumably. On the other hand Mel would, on past form, start out tender and brotherly, soon lose patience, start criticising, and move on smartly to carping and bullying; and Benny would get into various corresponding states, defiant and sullen, defiant and tearful, crushed, drunken, doped, or entirely collapsed. Still turning Mel down and just staying quietly on the dole would surely be a short cut to the whole lot, but bypassing the initial bout of good cheer.

'That's, that's marvellous!' said Marion warmly.

'I knew you'd be pleased,' said Benny, grinning. 'You could come and meet me now and then, if you like. At the nice places. Like before.'

Marion was silent. Once, long ago it seemed now, she had caught a ferry to Ireland, and spent a weekend with Benny, on tour in Dublin. Of all her life, her girl's life, her pre-Lewis-looking-for-romance life, it was the peak, and had stayed so, even now, when she had learnt to cope with Benny rather than to love him.

He had met her off the ferry and they had spent the afternoon wandering those graceful dingy streets, stopping in warm smoky bars, where men drank and played real music all day long. In the evening, Benny, drunk with love and Guinness, had sung to her; a scene scarcely credible to her now, but there it was, he had got up, and whispered to the man with the violin, come back to sit beside her and in that crowded bar, to an apparently unsurprised and unembarrassed audience of regulars, sung aloud a Victorian ballad, his grandma's party piece, he'd told her afterwards. His voice had been such a shock to her, so gentle and silvery, nothing like his harsh Americanised stage voice.

'Tis the last rose of summer, left blooming alone,
    All her lovely companions are faded and gone . . .'

The bar had grown quieter and quieter around him as more and more punters stopped talking to listen.

'When friendships have perished, and loved ones have flown,
Ah, who would inhabit this harsh world alone?'

He had sung it to her, looking into her eyes, which, despite her urgent and continuing embarrassment at him suddenly behaving like a musical, had at last filled and overflowed; and finished to cheers and friendly applause; and presently the fiddler had started something else, something home-grown and foot-tapping, and left them alone in the crowd.

And the following night had been so unforgettably thrilling: the theatre crammed with fans, people leaping up and down in their seats, sweating and whooping, bawling the words of the songs along with Mel, berserk with enthusiasm not only for Mel himself but for Smithie on drums, and Pete on bass guitar, and my old mate Benny, so Mel had called him, his hand on Benny's shoulder, my old mate Benny May on lead guitar—his words drowned out with cheers. And Marion, entranced in the wings, behind the staggering glare of the lights, had been dizzy with excitement and adoration.

Who were all those people out there, bouncing in their seats, and buying up the T-shirts and tapes and CDs? She had never heard of Mel or his band before meeting Benny. She had never known anyone connected with any kind of performance, no actors, no singers, no one in dance or the arts; that Benny had once known furious success, had been met at airports by hordes of girls all screeching; that he had appeared on posters, gentle-eyed, hair like Jesus, seventeen years old, and stripped to the waist; that he had once had more money than he knew how to spend: it was all too much for her, far too much.

She would have fallen in love with him without his past – his present then had been more than enough. His past, the drifts of cuttings, the hilarious back numbers of *Fab 208*, the mid-section pull-outs from *Jackie*, the lapel badges with Mel Springer 1970 printed over Benny's beautiful childish face, were just icing on the cake of his perfect exoticism.

'Couldn't we? Meet up?'

'I don't see how. What would I do with Lewis?' Marion spoke rather sharply. It was irritating to be reminded of Dublin, it was shabby behaviour, bringing all that up, she felt.

'Well, I don't know. Perhaps he'd be eating by then, it wouldn't be until summer, perhaps my mum could take him—'

'You've got to be joking.'

'She'd love to, I asked her.'

'Oh, come on, she couldn't. He wouldn't let her for a start. Didn't ask your dad, did you? Did you?'

'Well, no.'

'He goes mad if Lewis so much as moves, you know he does.'

And your mum's no better, Marion nearly added, but something kept her quiet. Before Lewis, and when he was tiny, she had felt rather sympathetic towards Benny's mother; it was clear that the main business of her life was trying to predict and avert her husband's rages. It had taken Marion some time to realise that she did so in order to protect herself rather than anyone else, and that, if bullying is the norm, everyone wants a try at it now and then, even the most doormat-like.

One time Lewis had had yoghurt on his jumper, the merest stain, you could hardly see it, but she'd been onto it like a flash, pouncing:

'I'm afraid he's not quite tidy, dear, is he. I do like him to be tidy when he comes to see us.'

I could see her finger trembling as she pointed, with her own daring: as if she were being her husband for a while, trying it on to see what it felt like. Bet she thought the less of herself too, for not enjoying it as much as he seems to.

She couldn't meet my eyes afterwards. It was me taking that twenty quid off her, for his snowsuit: gave her the right, she must have thought. And then she just had to use it, I don't suppose she gets the chance that often.

'She won't even move the ornaments,' said Marion, aloud. 'I mean, all she has to do is put everything out of his reach. Those sodding china squirrels.'

'He's got to learn to behave!' Benny's father, purple-faced, letting them all have it. And his mum cooing, pretending that nothing was happening, no one was roaring, that was her method when her prediction-and-avoidance tactics failed, as they so frequently did.

They're both just nutters, concluded Marion dismally, again. But it's nurture, not nature, she reminded herself. They may have had free rein with Benny, but they're not getting their hands on Lewis.

Not for a whole weekend. Not for more than two hours once a fortnight. With me there keeping an eye on them too. Because Benny's dad was shameless.

'So what's a nice girl like you doing with this fat has-been?' he had asked Marion, at their second or third meeting; gleefully, gloves off. This is Us, he had been saying, as if proudly.

'Leaving,' she said, taking Benny's hand and leading him away never to darken their doors again.

That's what I should have done.

Nah. What's the use, I could never have done anything anyway, no one could, it's always been much too late.

'Leaving!'

Wish I had though.

'What about your mother then?'

'What? Oh. Well. Maybe. We'll see. Nearer the time, okay?' Marion felt suddenly light-headed with sleepiness. 'Look, I'm just going to shut my eyes, I'm just—' She yawned, turned sideways. The window vibrated against her cheek. I'll never sleep like this, she just had time to think, before she fell asleep.

93

Benny, left alone, fumbled for a minute or two in the cassette box, and put a tape on, nothing like the usual sort of thing he listened to, but one lent him by someone in his therapy group, a lot of voices making a sound that was somehow distinctly circular, graceful, like a big skirt; it was there in the back of his mind, a skirt as big as a merry-go-round, revolving, dipping. He hummed along to it, swaying a little in his seat, trying to move in the same flowing circles.

Very nice, he thought, as the chorus ended. Still. He flicked it off. Classical stuff: you couldn't listen to it for long, it made you gloomy, it was all about the past, it was all about death. He found something else more his style, waggled the headphones on one-handed, and pushed the volume up so that the sound went right through him.

Alive, alive, said the beat. Alive now. Sex-music, by, with or from sex, Mel had said, laughing, twenty years ago now. Still true.

The words were as fiercely sexual as the beat, *Gonna get you girl, gonna take you, make you mine* . . .

Benny sang along with them, take it, make it, his voice unconsciously tender, in his private, silvery, gentle tenor.

Take it, make it!

The drums thundered in his head.

Benny's whole body seemed to yearn to the rhythm, with a tense abandonment, the closest he could ever come to relaxation while sober.

11

ANNIE, PUSHING OPEN THE DOOR OF HER FLAT, SAW his handwriting immediately, lying there on the floor looking up at her. Her heart stopped beating, then seemed to fall over itself trying to catch up. She put her hand to her chest, coughing, then tried some deep breaths, but for a minute or two it went on beating irregularly, pausing for what felt like several seconds at a time and then fluttering as if in a panic.

I'm dying, thought Annie in terror, but the idea of having a fatal seizure at the mere sight of Peter's handwriting was hard to take seriously even in extremis, and made it possible not to take the fluttering heartbeats seriously either. It's all in the mind, she told herself. It's nothing to worry about, I know, it's palpitations, it's something silly people bore their GPs with.

Firmly she stepped over the letter and the other mail and went to the kitchen, where after a few minutes' peering and scrabbling she came up with a little bottle of brandy. Dubiously she looked at the label. Why did they always make out Napoleon drank it, what was that supposed to prove? Shopped at Tesco's, did he? she asked the label jeeringly as she poured the stuff into an egg-cup. Her heart was still juddering and bouncing. She sniffed at the egg-cup and an ancient memory of adolescence, of catastrophic public drunkenness and a consequential week-long hang-over, was instantly, queasily vivid, as if it had been only yesterday and not fifteen years before, that fifth-form notoriety: Annie Grey, oh, that's her, it was her that was sick in a birdbath—

Andrew Greenslade's parents' birdbath, thought Annie now, sniffing again. God, it smelt like lighter fuel, of wretched nausea and embarrassment. The Girl Who Was Sick In A Birdbath, that's me for life, for some people. Never touched spirits since. Wasn't that a bit pathetic, really? Annie held her nose with one hand and tossed the stuff back with the other.

'Blech!'

It worked though – by the time she stopped coughing and retching her heart was definitely back to normal, beating rapidly but at least in time. Annie laughed a little as she wiped her eyes. She felt rather triumphant, having laid the ghost of the birdbath if nothing else. Now for that bastard's letter.

Dear Annie—

There were photographs, two of them. Annie laid them aside.

I thought you might like to have these. Do you remember that weekend? I've been thinking and thinking about what you said. I would like to see you but as nothing has changed I suppose you feel we have nothing to talk about.

Love, Peter

The photographs, taken that summer, showed Annie sitting on a stone plinth pretending to be a statue, and the green pretty view from the bedroom window of the pub where they had stayed.

Dear Annie, thought Annie, translating. I thought these photographs would make you feel extra miserable, so here they are. We were so happy that weekend, and you have thrown us away. I love you but not enough to marry you. I miss you but I'm too craven to say so, and I insist you take the blame for all this.

And Love, Peter.

Annie got up and paced to and fro in the kitchen, too disgusted to keep still. Was this really the best he could come up with?

I suppose you feel we have nothing to talk about— Too right, thought Annie scornfully. You certainly had nothing to write about, did you?

And that was the ploy, she thought, giving me a few lines so that I can read all sorts of things in between them, things he can always some day claim weren't there. He wants me to wonder if there's hope for us, because wondering and hoping makes you weak.

What to do? Tear everything up, send it all back in bits? No, too melodramatic, and reminiscent, as well, of What-shername, Hester, and Chapter Two, it would be ridiculous, hordes of women sending him vengeful packets of little shreds – Annie giggled. No, obviously it was best to do nothing, let him feel his silly letter had been posted into the void. Let him lie awake at night wondering if she'd even got it at all.

Let him, eventually, have to ring up to find out.

Feeling hard and cheerfully excited Annie made herself some cheese on toast, and took out her copy of the latest government health-service shake-up, meaning to have another go at it. Someone was surely going to ask her opinion of it sooner or later, and facetious comments on its possible uses as a doorstop or, rolled up tightly with string, as a traditional blunt instrument, would cut no ice at the office.

But it was very hard going, and phrases from Peter's letter kept inserting themselves as she read. And after a bite or so the toast had a curious glossy inedible look to it, as if it were one of those clever plastic facsimiles attached to key-rings.

97

Annie sat back and lit a cigarette. Phone someone? No. There was, she thought, a strong chance of her ending up in tears if she tried. Visit Marion? That was always good for morale. But no: this weekend even Marion was having a better time than she was, off to the country en famille, visiting someone or other from Benny's dim and distant, the Ghost Of Glamrock Past, Marion had called him; she was looking forward to it, somewhere in the country, all Essex-man palatial, she said, a rock-star's dream home, circular beds, guitar-shaped swimming pool, baths on podiums, black silk sheets . . .

From this pleasant fantasy Annie drifted suddenly into a memory, of lying in her own bed early one day when she and Peter were very new and joyful. She had been there alone that morning, dozing, and she had turned, and caught his particular smell on the sheet, and felt an immediate vivid impression of his whole body, so real that, though it lasted barely a second, she could still remember that instant hallucinatory sense of his weight and the feel of his skin beneath her fingers. It was the sort of thing animals might feel, she had thought at the time, a sense normally denied to humans, a kind of physical picturing.

Through this memory, Annie, still clutching her ciga-rette, felt a sudden strong pull of sexual desire, and jumped a little in her chair from surprise; she was not used to such explicit signals. And recovering found herself alone with nothing but an unconvincing letter and photographs sent to pain her. Every effort at control seemed to fail at once. The charge nurse turned and looked at her, mocking all love.

Annie put the cigarette out, and her head down on the doorstop government health-service shake-up, and began ashamedly to cry.

18

MARION LAY COSILY ON THE BED WITH LEWIS, listening to the talk from the table in the room below her. It was pleasant to have a reasonable excuse for Lewis.

'He's a bit difficult in places he doesn't know—' Implying, of course, that he was a little angel in places he did, a fiction Marion herself found not only very comforting but plausible, even convincing: bearing the other tranquil Lewis in mind she had rather more patience than usual with the real one, as if this present vehement refusal to go to sleep really was a one-off, and not at all his usual nightly performance.

And downstairs everything was really very jolly, and civilised, Mel still touchingly doing his best; he'd been really glad to see them and absolutely crackers about Lewis, asking straight away if he could hold him and going on and on about his looks, and playing with him, trying to make him laugh, succeeding.

'Oh, I want one like this. What d'you think, Soph? Should we have one like this? Just a little one?'

And Sophie, the newish girlfriend, had been a pleasant surprise, seemed simply nice and ordinary, ordinary to look at anyway, even a bit scruffy, with hair that was evidently just combed now and then, and sitting presently at the table in a dim floral item that made Marion's own well-worn blue look positively chic. And she had the wrong shoes on.

The only real snag had been the house. There was something immediately uncomfortable about it, Marion had thought at first. As if the place were haunted. Mel had showed them all round, the new wooden floors, the extra staircase, the new fitted cupboards in the bedrooms.

'That's new? That one?'

Everything looked as if it had always been there. Marion was confused. She had not known, she realised, that reproduction could simply be reproduction, and not some kind of pretence. The cupboard in this little eighteenth-century room was the sort of cupboard eighteenth-century builders might have made, and the windows in the new dayroom were mullioned in local stone.

'Clever, isn't it?' Mel had said. 'It all looks the same age. Sophie's doing, not mine. I wouldn't have known what to ask for. Designed the whole thing, didn't you, Soph?'

Marion would have liked to know whether all this designing took place before or after Sophie had moved in, not only out of simple prurience but also because Sophie turning out to be some sort of professional architect or something would be reassuring, something to hang onto in the face of not having known about mullions. On their way down the new, beautiful, oak staircase she had asked, tentatively, if Sophie had done this sort of thing before, and been vexed by Sophie's answering giggle, Oh gosh no, it had been a nightmare, it was like the gasman cometh, plasterers breaking windows and glaziers gouging plaster, frankly never again, actually.

Worst of all was the kitchen, which was entirely new, finished just that week, Sophie had said.

'We didn't want a fitted kitchen. I think they're so soulless—'

'Yes, yes,' said Marion eagerly, forgetting how often she had sighed over the advertisements in the womens' maga-

100

zines, yearning for the full treatment from Smallbones of Devizes.

Not much cupboard space though.

'And anyway there's enough room for a separate pantry over there, you see. And a sort of dirty boot entrance; it gets terribly muddy in winter—'

Separate stone-flagged scullery too, with an enormous shallow trough-like sink beside the sleek German washing-machine. At the sight of that sink Marion had felt her heart turn into something similarly cold and weighty.

Above the sink ran three long wooden poles, with saddles sitting on them.

'Got a couple of horses in the paddock,' said Mel, as Benny fingered one of them. 'Fancy a ride tomorrow? Don't laugh, Sophie's teaching me,' he added, seeing Benny's face. 'Aren't you, Soph?'

'Trying to.'

'Get away, I'm brilliant—'

'He is utterly useless.'

'Flaming cheek—' Mel squeezed her against him, lifting her from the ground. 'And we've got sheep, come and see the sheep, they're called If and But—'

The sheep were in the orchard, beside the walled kitchen garden. Lewis had fought to reach them, struggling in Mel's arms.

'And look, see the horses? There, look!'

'It's a real flower meadow, we'll be making organic hay—'

Released, Lewis stumbled amongst the damp fallen leaves.

'Little red apples, they are, all crunchy, no one knows what they are, it's such an old tree, the rest are Bramleys though. This one's a crab. And one Russet over there.'

The walls of the kitchen garden were lined with peach trees. 'And this one's a medlar, I'd never even seen a medlar, you eat them with cheese apparently, when they've practically gone bad—'

'In the spring', said Sophie happily, 'there was so much blossom. All the washing smelt of apple blossom.'

Marion saw her, breathing in her clean sheets at the washing line beside the orchard, and felt that she could bear no more.

'Um, I think you, yes, sorry, he needs a new nappy, come on you, yes, we'll see the horses again in a minute—' and she escaped, to give herself a talking-to.

Now look. They are just pleased with it all. Not flaunting. It's me, not them. I didn't really know what money could buy. Or: I thought riches always meant ostentation.

It's as if they've bought England. Old England. And there is nothing I can look down on, that's the real trouble. I mean, I always knew he was loaded, but—

But. Marion sighed. She had not realised how much she had banked on snobbery as a refuge from jealousy. Where was the white leather furniture, the mirrors over the king-sized beds, the en-suite jacuzzis she had, she saw, been quite gleefully looking forward to? How could she have got Mel so wrong?

And would anyone feel like this, or was she simply an unusually nasty person? Already, watching Mel showing Lewis the sheep, she had caught herself remembering, as a comfort, that like Annie, so upwardly mobile Annie, Mel and Sophie so far had no baby. That was unusually nasty all right.

'Shall we have one like this, just a small one?' Look at the fuss he had made of Lewis, holding him, playing with him. This was a place to bring up children, that's what he bought it for, that's what he wants. Soberly Marion looked into herself, and saw there a certain small hope that in this desire Mel would be thwarted.

Shaming, and frightening. There lay Lewis, so little and fragile. He could easily be taken away from her; she would deserve it, for having such thoughts. And he wouldn't be childless on his own, would he; what had Sophie ever done to her, apart from owning a stone sink and sheets scented with apple blossom, to warrant ill-wishing on such a scale?

In any case if anyone really had cause to be jealous it was obviously Benny, not her. It could have been his, all this. He'd had the money once. And spent it, poor soul, alternately on drugs and cures, on things chosen not, it seemed, to lessen his unhappiness but merely to demonstrate it, as messily as possible.

Though of course all that had been very fashionable in those days. If you looked at the early posters and album covers Mel and the others looked like alternate drug/cure spendthrifts as well, the clothes all the same brand of rock-star ragbag, their expressions also dated and uniform, a curious combination of slackness and menace, the unsmiling mock-challenge: nothing further can rouse me, said the face of the times, and to everyone's anxious mum and dad: everything you fear about us is true.

Was it any kind of virtue in Benny that with him this pose had been more or less valid? Or were there any grounds there for despising Mel, who had evidently been saying something very different all along to respectable brokers and building societies?

'Okay?' Benny stood in the doorway.

'Just a bit wet, that's all,' said Marion, snapping the last popper to.

Benny sat down beside her on the bed, which creaked beneath his weight, and Lewis put out a hand to touch his father's cheek.

'Hallo, scrumptious. What a place, eh.'

'Did you know it would be like this?'

'Like what?' said Benny, anxiously.

'I don't know, erm, classy, I suppose.'

'He's turning into a country gent,' said Benny. 'He's got green wellies, and one of those wax jackets.'

'No.' They grinned into one another's faces.

'Riding a horse!'

'Heh heh heh!'

103

'What's next, fox-hunting, otter-hounds?'

'Her dad keeps foxhounds,' said Benny. 'Sophie's dad.'

'Really? What, you mean—'

'And her mum breeds spaniels.'

'What a lot of dogs,' said Marion in cockney, 'must be bleeding noisy, their house.' They sniggered.

'There's a stuffed one downstairs, fox's head, did you see it? One of her dad's, he's got dozens apparently, done up all snarling and ferocious, this teeny little fox, I mean, really scary if you're a mouse or a gerbil or something—'

'Yuk.' But of course they would have to make it snarl and be wild, thought Marion, or it would look just like a small beheaded dog there on the wall. 'Does Sophie do it, go hunting?'

'I didn't ask . . . they're getting married.'

'I thought so, didn't you?'

'Well, no, actually. I never saw him getting married.'

'He wants babies. Because you've got one.'

Benny smiled shyly. 'Oh, I don't think it's that. He was telling me just now, when she'd gone to get the tea on: he's a bit worried actually. That he can't.'

'No, don't touch that, give it to mummy, thank you, is he, why's that?'

'Well, he's taken a lot of risks, you know, for years. No one's ever got, well, pregnant. And they've been trying, him and Sophie, for ages, he says, getting on for a year.'

Yes, thought Marion. It was obvious now. Sophie had not yet once touched Lewis. Not out of carefree lack of interest after all then, but from something much more painful. She could not bear to touch him, thought Marion.

'And her as well, she had this really bad appendicitis when she was a kid apparently, she got peritonitis, that could, you know, bugger things up as well. They've got to try for a year though, before they get looked at, you know, doctors.'

'Oh. How old is she?'

'Thirty.'

104

'Oh dear.'

'Nice place for a kid, this.'

He'd thought of it too then: let Mel be thwarted. Marion looked away, lest their eyes meet. Only for a little while, thought Marion at the Fates. Just let him be worried about it for a little while. Nothing more than that. Honest.

'Still wants to go on tour though. He's being very nice to me.'

'Why shouldn't he be?' She had turned, and given him a quick kiss. 'Let's hope he keeps it up.'

And so he had, so far.

Friday evening had passed very pleasantly, and this morning Mel and Benny had gone off for a long walk, taking Lewis with them, crowing in the backpack, and Marion had fallen back into bed and slept for another deep peaceful four hours, and then Sophie had knocked on the door with a mug of real coffee.

'Oh, thank you, oh, what luxury!'

'Um, I gave Lewis a banana, is that all right?'

'What, you mean he ate it?'

'Yes. I gave it to him whole, that's how my nephew likes them.'

'Oh.'

'Is that all right?'

'Yes, yes of course—' Marion had closed her eyes for pleasure. Greedily she thought of the banana, its clean packeted load of minerals, vitamins, and carbohydrate, all now sustaining her child.

'Benny said he was a bit difficult.'

'He doesn't eat very well,' said Marion lightly, implying that otherwise he was very little trouble, for it seemed to her that to mention the trials of motherhood, even in passing, to someone yearning for a baby would be subtly unkind, and possibly construed as some clumsy attempt at consolation. Or even as a conscious piece of cruelty, the sort of thing an unusually nasty person would go in for.

But then making out he was an angel might look like just the same thing.

'He's all right,' she added weakly, but oh dear, mightn't sounding offhand be rather insulting as well?

'I think you're marvellous, breast-feeding him so long,' said Sophie. 'My sister couldn't manage it at all, and David was allergic to cows' milk protein, he got the most awful eczema, he had to go to hospital at one point.'

'How awful.'

'She's really determined this time, she's pregnant again you see, she's coming over for supper tonight, I mean they are; I wonder, would you mind sort of giving her a bit of advice, what worked for you? She wants to be able to try everything, you see, and you're obviously really good at it.'

'Well, of course. Of course I will.'

'And would it be all right if I took Lewis to the barn with me? I thought he might like to give Spray a carrot, she's very gentle and used to children. You could have a bath, if you liked, there's lots of hot water. While I looked after him. Would that be all right?'

It had all been like that, thought Marion now, shifting Lewis over to the other side and stroking the soft pale fluff of his head: a whole day of other people gently taking the baby away to amuse him, while she did other small delightfully nostalgic things: ate breakfast while looking at the paper; blew-dry her hair; applied body lotion; chatted idly with Sophie about diets, and learnt that Sophie's sister, poor thing, had hardly lost an ounce since David's birth, and put it down to bottle-feeding.

'I mean I'm sure that's why you're so slim,' Sophie had added, and then they had had a very interesting discussion about body image, self-esteem, and eventually bust-size, the mechanics and desirability of achieving a cleavage, and someone Sophie knew who'd had plastic surgery followed by shift and seepage, and ended up for a while with something like a bosom just under one arm.

A holiday really, the first since Lewis was born. And

106

inside Lewis, right now, an entire second banana was gently digesting. And he was asleep. Wasn't he? Marion half rose, waiting for him to snap his eyes open as usual when she moved away, but his breathing did not change. Holding her breath herself she picked him up and laid him carefully in his travel-cot. He did not stir. Eating and sleeping! Had he made it then, finally reached the turning-point all the doctors and health visitors kept coming up with, Oh, he'll be all right, he'll suddenly take off, he'll catch up, you'll see—

Two whole bananas! As she considered them, gloatingly, a sudden low undulating whistle sounded from outside, making her jump, but even before it had died away she realised what it must be. Might she see it, perhaps, the owl in the garden? As quietly as possible Marion crept to the window, and opened it to the clear, cool night air. A heavy smell of leaves and earth, delicious; Marion leant out, snuffing it, through the new eighteenth-century lattice. She waited for the owl to call again.

There was no moon, so it was the dim light from behind the closed dining-room curtains that showed her Mel and Benny, standing by the side door, evidently taking the air, as she was. Forgetting all about the owl she raised a hand, meaning to call down to them, but as she did so something about the way they were standing checked her. She waited, puzzled, while her heart began to pound painfully in her stomach as she leant against the window-sill.

Speak to them. Show them you're here. Go on. Why don't you?

Their voices were very low, too low for her to make out a word. What could Mel be saying, so close to Benny's ear?

Quick, say something, now!

But still she waited, and presently the murmur stopped, and Mel bent his head, for a long, sexual kiss. There was Benny's hand on his shoulder, holding him.

Too late.

Slowly Marion drew her head in, leaving the window

where it was, in case it caught the light and betrayed her. For a moment she sat completely still, feeling only her own heartbeat. Then words broke in:

Well of course.

Obviously.

All this time.

Ever since.

She shivered, it was cold sitting there by the open window. Presently came the sound of the door opening and closing, and she risked a look out, and they had gone.

Marion closed the window carefully, making no sound, and after a little while judged that the trembling was going off, and that she could manage things, for a time, given the number of other people about and the ordinary talk there would be. She took out her comb, and for a few minutes sat in the darkness, slowly drawing it through her hair.

A sudden burst of laughter sounded from downstairs. They were all having a lovely time down there. Ordinary talk: she longed for it. She put the comb back in her toilet bag, zipped it up, put her shoes back on, checked Lewis, fast asleep, the stranger's child, and at last went down to join them.

19

TONIGHT STANLEY WAS MAKING MARMALADE, BUT since the wildlife programme started at 7.10, he had transferred operations to the living room; though after last week's baby pelicans he was fully prepared to switch smartly off again. You could never relax with wildlife programmes, he had found, though tonight's looked fairly harmless: it was hard to get too upset about fish.

He dug his knife into his second hot, soft lemon. The mush inside stung his fingers, and his glasses kept misting up, but the smell was delicious and just as he remembered. Keep this half for shredding, and mince that one. Pips in the hanky. See? Easy, isn't it, he almost-thought at Amy, who would have fussed, certainly, at his doing this sort of thing on the living-room carpet, but look at all this news-paper, he explained. And the mats on the largest nesting-table, it'll be all right, you'll see.

On the screen microscopic organisms, starred like snow-flakes, revolved in water as thick as syrup. Stanley thought immediately of Hitler. Bet he's come back as one of those. Bet he's been a shrimp-like arthropod, eaten alive over and over again in the Arctic seas beneath the ice, thought Stanley cheerfully, and serve him right.

He started to slice an orange, and the doorbell made him jump and shoot a pip onto the hearthrug.

'Now who can that be?' he asked the television, but turned it down before going to find out.

'Oh, hallo!'

'Hallo Dad. How are you?'

'What have you done to your hair?'

'Can't I come in?'

''Course you can—'

'You should have seen it three weeks ago,' said Peter excitedly.

'Um—' said Stanley. He felt slightly irritated. 'Look, come on through, I'm just—'

'What on earth are you doing?'

'What does it look like, look, d'you mind if I, it won't be on long, they take you right under the ice—'

'Oh, I see, well, no, of course not.'

Peter sat down, without taking his coat off. For a moment, given his general state of mind and the three pints of bitter he had drunk on the way, he felt almost ready to cry.

'So long as it stays fish,' said Stanley, putting the volume up again.

Peter leant back and closed his eyes. Get a grip, he told himself. 'Want a hand, then?'

'Oh, erm—' A startled bream was gathering up her babies, a thousand valiantly swimming mites, into her own huge mouth for safe keeping. 'Look at that! Yes, all right, thanks—' One had got left behind, and was toiling all alone in the thick water, to and fro, as if hopefully, before her great unblinking eye. 'Get yourself a knife, you'll need a plate as well,' called Stanley, as Peter trailed off into the kitchen.

He picked up his piece of orange, still watching. Damn: back on dry land again. And birds as well; and last week's baby pelicans waddled desolately across his mind once more.

I'll turn it off, he promised himself, as Peter came back in again. Looking a bit peaky, more than a bit, really, though perhaps that was the haircut.

110

'Take your coat off, son.'

Hardly a mention, Peter was thinking almost bitterly. And all that yapping years ago, What the hell do you think you look like? You look like a girl, you're not coming to your nan's like that, I won't be seen out with you—

And it's so pretty too, honestly Peter, natural ringlets, it's not fair—

That had been Annabel, beautiful Annabel, Joe's Annabel, pretending to be jealous. She could sit on her hair, golden brown, plaited into pre-Raphaelite masses. Everyone had long hair then.

'I can sit on my hair.' Demure Annabel. 'But it's terribly dull. Come over here, Peter, and let me sit on yours.'

'Can you just slice these up? Like this?'

'I know. I've done it before.'

'Have you?' asked Stanley, but with his eyes on the screen.

For a while they chopped and sliced in silence, while half-grown guillemots, too big now for their nests, launched themselves into their first flights, to glide eight hundred metres into the safety of the sea, or ('Not again,' said Stanley, wincing) to get it just slightly wrong, and fall short, gliding instead into the waiting jaws of dozens of Arctic foxes.

'Oh dear,' said Peter flatly, hoping to sound uninterested in the television rather than slighted by its being on in the first place, but Stanley appeared not to notice either possibility, clutching his knife in tense silence while the birds lined up and leapt into space one by one. After a few days the Arctic foxes were full, it seemed, and lolled about on the pebbles, snapping idly at the newest casualties, some of whom were then able to struggle past them into the breakers.

'I don't know why you watch this stuff,' said Peter, as another one just made it home-free.

'Sometimes it's lovely, the colours and everything,' said Stanley, relaxing as the credits rolled. 'You should have

111

seen last week's,' he said, getting up to switch off. 'It was awful.' He hesitated.

'Oh?' Actually it was rather soothing, slicing lemon peel, Peter thought. 'Is this fine enough?'

'Where? Oh yes, anyway it was these pelicans—'

'Yeah.'

'They're born too late in the breeding season, second batch, see. And the lake dries up, and the parents fly away, they have to, there's nothing to eat, they circle around and then they just fly away. And the baby ones can't fly.'

'Oh?'

'Yes,' said Stanley, sitting down. 'And they all wander about together, the baby ones, a whole crowd of them, and then they just start walking—'

'Gawd.'

'—off into the desert. There's nowhere to go, it's miles to the nearest water-hole. They all die, one by one. I could hardly stand to watch it, you know, I kept thinking, if they can film it why can't they do something, scoop 'em up, carry them—'

Peter kept his head bent, for it was his mother talking.

'—and it was on so early, children could've seen it, they don't want to know about that sort of thing,' said Stanley indignantly. A herd of little Charlie Chaplins, that's what they'd looked like, barely able to master their great flat feet. And their helpless parents, circling, calling, he had felt for them, too. 'And the commentator, he was just lapping it up, you know, this is Nature for you, "On this march of death",' Stanley sneered. Though he felt a bit better about it at the moment, he noticed suddenly.

'Want a cup of tea?'

'Please.'

Peter sat back. His fingers were beginning to ache. Did it happen every year, the holocaust of baby pelicans? He stirred in his armchair, remembering the white rhinos he had seen a fortnight earlier, alone in his flat with the television and a six-pack of lager from the supermarket.

112

The rhinos, being saved from a new reservoir, had been stunned with tranquillisers, slung in giant hammocks suspended beneath helicopters, and flown hundreds of miles over the savannah, was it? to safety somewhere else.

What had rather drunkenly bothered Peter at the time was the question of how the rhinos had coped with the sensation of flight, whether, snorting about in their new homes, they had been troubled by urgent dreams and flashbacks of weightlessness and rushing air. They had looked so patient hanging in their hammocks, so vulnerable with their big armoured legs dangling. They would surely be quite unable to make sense of their memories.

The earth fell away and left me behind.

A great bird took me.

I was turned into a bird, and flew.

That was the sort of thing they might have come up with: stories, miracles of transformation. The fount of all such human myths, perhaps, thought Peter now, sucking his sticky fingers: a completely skewed but honest attempt to describe events no one could understand. And no one has such adventures any more, he thought, we see icebergs, not miraculous columns of floating crystal, and geological fault-lines, not Poseidon. Only animals can have such adventures now. And then because of us by and large, saved or butchered they are passive in our hands.

Then his mind seemed to jump, as if all by itself, made him sit up and nearly knock his nesting-table over, Oh Annie, oh I miss you—

'Here we are,' said Stanley. He put a tray down carefully on the carpet. 'Now then. How are you? Sorry about that, it was last week's, I think I wanted to take the taste away.'

'Nah, you're an addict.'

'I just can't understand how they do it, get in so close and everything. Biscuit?'

'Thanks. Perhaps they shouldn't, though. I mean, there's nowhere safe from us, is there? from our prying eyes. And when you think of the things we get to see—' he trailed off.

All those mysteries laid bare week after week, he thought, for us to sip tea over, not just the privacies of animals but the processes within them, the tremulous parting of chromosomes, the fusion of alien cells; suppose we were only being allowed it, this God's-eye-view, because it was all coming to an end. Look, God or Life or something-or-other might be saying, Look, at these different parallel worlds, in detail and in general, this was here all along, while you were chucking crude oil on it, or open-cast mining on it, or spraying it with herbicide. See it? Say goodbye.

'You all right?'

Peter shrugged. And always showing them fucking, he thought. That was suspicious in itself, not liberal so much as tabloid in intent. All part of the fairground fun, watch dungbeetles or hippos or puffins in the act of copulation, why was that all right when you couldn't show people at it? Besides so much was always left out. If the strongest lion got all the lionesses, what happened to the weaker ones? You got such a cock-eyed picture, it was only the strong ones they showed you, sleeping and eating and fucking all day; somewhere out there, surely, were hundreds of less successful lions never getting any sex at all.

'Just a bit tired, I suppose.'

'Annie all right?'

Ritual enquiries.

'Yeah, fine, thanks.'

'And Joe?'

'In the pink.'

'Still not seeing anyone?' said Stanley, lifting the lid of the teapot.

Peter shook his head. There was a pause. He remembered remembering Annabel's beautiful hair.

'Did you ever meet Annabel?' he asked.

Stanley looked up, considering. 'No. Don't think so.'

Wish I hadn't. Wish Joe hadn't.

'You'd have remembered.'

114

'Would I? Your mother thought—' Stanley looked away. 'Your mother thought you blamed yourself a bit.'

'Did she? No. It wasn't anyone's fault. I mean I wish, I used to wish I'd happened to look in sooner. But I didn't, that's all.'

'It was a rotten thing to happen. To a lad your age.'

'It didn't happen to me,' said Peter, 'did it, it happened to Annabel.'

'Yes, yes, all right, I know, I shouldn't have mentioned it—'

'It's Joe got fucked up by it, not me. Sorry.'

Knocking on her bedroom door, whispering, 'Annabel? Annabel?' and pushing it gently open, not seeing her yet in the dim light.

Peter got up, wanting to stride about, but there were bowls and plates of oranges and lemons all over the place, he had to keep looking where he was going.

Holding his breath, undressing, to slip in beside her and wake her, pounce surprise!

Peter stood still, and closed his eyes, the better to concentrate on not remembering what had happened next.

Opened them: 'Actually I'm not seeing Annie any more.'

'Aren't you?'

'Nope. All for the best. I expect.'

Peter's indifferent tone irritated Stanley very much. It did not occur to him that it might be assumed, for he no longer counted himself amongst those his son might wish to deceive. Whereas Peter, in the discomfort of the moment, had rather forgotten who he was talking to, and so was annoyed in his turn by his father's evident lack of sympathy, which proved to him yet again that his old dad was merely the chilly self-righteous tyrant he had often seemed when Peter was seventeen.

He stiffened, waiting, bored already, for some freshly updated version of the I-don't-know-what-you-young-people-are-coming-to speech Stanley had inflicted on everyone so often for so long.

115

While Stanley, who had in fact long ago accepted that Peter's behaviour, though regrettable, was hardly out of the ordinary, if the messy goings-on of most of his own contemporaries' children, getting divorced and having children out of wedlock all over the place, was anything to go by, told himself that there was no point any longer in trying to make his real views known. His son was heartless; the fashions of the times made him a user of women. Well, thought Stanley, surely sooner or later all these silly girls would wake up to the truth. He remembered Annie with tenderness now, forgetting what a frightening virago he had generally thought her whenever they had met.

He sat up and began piling the cold fruit together on his tray.

'Well,' he said at last. 'I don't want to meet any more of them. If you don't mind. That's all.' He got up, rather stiffly, perhaps a little more stiffly than was strictly necessary, and went away to the kitchen, from which resolutely placid clinking jam-making noises presently emerged.

Peter, deflated and obscurely ashamed of himself, could think of nothing better to do than wonder if the *News* was on yet. After a minute or two he went over, and switched on to find out.

20

THE CONCERT WAS ONLY TWO WEEKS AWAY NOW.

'And frankly I think we should sound rather better than this,' said Mrs Downely, changing the record, 'because they take this movement too slowly, it really needs to go at a fair old lick, listen.'

Janet was a little drunk, for tonight Mrs Downely had opened a bottle of wine. She hummed along with her eyes closed.

'See? Drags its feet, doesn't it?'

'Well—'

'Perhaps the trouble with listening to music is that it is essentially an unnatural thing to do. And possibly quite new, as human activity goes. I mean sitting still not doing anything else, not even knitting, certainly not chatting. Don't you think so? Music surely was first made to pray to or to dance to. All those Haydn quartets, for instance, I'm sure they were really a sort of early Muzak, for aristocrats to have soirées to. And they'd be simply amazed to see people nowadays respectfully keeping quiet to it.'

Janet smiled. 'It's not a spectator sport then?'

'Well of course it's not, that's why we're all right, singing our heads off, it's the audience I'm sorry for, paying to be frustrated, that's what it amounts to. You stand in the foyer

117

when they come out, you listen to them. They will sound exhilarated, they'll be nattering away nineteen to the dozen, laughing like a party; it's because it's finished. I half believe that's why they come in the first place, to have the lovely relief of it all being over with.'

'That can't be right.'

'No, it can't, can it? Just a thought. Shall I top you up a little?'

'Thank you. What did you do? Before you retired?'

'I was a teacher,' said Mrs Downely, 'in a girls' school, surely it was obvious?' She named the school, but Janet, predictably, had never heard of it.

'Then I got married, and gave it up, one did in those days. Then I got divorced, which was rather unusual. Then I got married again. Which is why I own this rather grand flat, my second husband was quite wealthy.'

'Oh.'

'His name was Cecil, and he was a very nice chap. He was considerably older than I was, have you noticed that women always say that, of an elderly husband, considerably older? He could remember Queen Victoria's funeral; he used to say he had been held up to the window to watch her cortège pass by. I used to wonder if he wasn't actually remembering a scene from *Cavalcade*, a play where just this happens, but just because it happened in a play doesn't mean it didn't in real life, does it? I expect it happened all over London – *Cavalcade* was an immense success – perhaps there were elderly ladies and gentlemen, no, they would only have been middle-aged at the time, middle-aged Victorians then, sobbing in the stalls night after night, don't you? Oh, yes, that was me, held up to the window, yes, what a little lady she was! They must all have thought they'd said so. They should all have said so anyway, it was clearly the right thing to say. Shall we have the other side?'

'All right. I'm not working tomorrow.'

So graceless, thought Mrs Downely, without rancour. But it was an opening at last.

118

'What is your work?'

'I'm a theatre nurse. I do eye operations mostly.'

'Really. What strong nerves you must have.'

'You get used to it.'

'Are you a Staff Nurse or a Sister? Do they still have Sisters these days?'

'They do, but I'm not one, I can't be, I'm an Enrolled Nurse.'

'So you can't be promoted, is that right? I think they started the scheme up during the war, when they needed quantity rather than quality, is it still so?'

Janet shrugged.

'I didn't mean you, I'm sorry, I was just surprised. You see I've had quite a lot of practice judging these things, you're evidently quality rather than quantity, aren't you, why are you stuck at such a low grade? If that doesn't sound too unkind.'

Janet made no reply.

'It was too unkind.'

'No. It's true. I try not to think about it though.'

'Surely you could retrain, upgrade? If you wanted to?'

'I suppose so.'

'Of course, you've kept rather busy, haven't you, abandoning household items.'

Janet giggled into her wineglass.

'And of course they would make you do the whole thing all over again, wouldn't they, terribly tedious.'

'I don't know. I did start the SRN course. A long time ago.'

'Did you? And you gave it up?'

'Yes.'

'How depressing. Why?'

'They said the other one would be easier.'

'And why did they say that? Couldn't you manage the regular course?'

'Oh, it wasn't that.'

Mrs Downely waited, but not, she thought, too long.

119

'What was it, then?'

Janet sighed and wriggled, and gulped at her wine. Oh, poor thing, poor thing, thought Mrs Downely immediately, I should leave her alone, why should I make her tell me if she doesn't want to?

'I'm so sorry. I'm being nosy.'

'Yes, you are, aren't you. I don't mind. I'm always telling people anyway. I got into trouble, I got pregnant, my boyfriend didn't want to know and my father threw me out. I had the baby in a mother-and-baby home. In Essex. He was adopted. When I came back they said the SRN course might be a bit too much for me and I'd lost so much time anyway why didn't I swap and do the SEN, it would be easier. So I did.'

'Oh,' said Mrs Downely. 'Well, I suppose I did ask.'

There was a pause.

'Shall I play the last side? It's quite exciting, even to just listen to.'

'I don't mind.'

'They were punishing you, weren't they?'

'I don't know. D'you think so?'

'Maybe not consciously. I'm sure they told themselves they were being tremendously broad-minded and liberal and helpful and so on. When did all this happen? Do you mind talking about it?'

Janet shrugged again. 'Not really. It was 1970.'

'But it is such an old story!'

'What d'you mean?'

'It happened right at the end, right at the—' Mrs Downely gestured, words failing her for a moment. 'I mean that things have changed, so much, so quickly, it is an archaic story, it almost need not have happened, you're like, oh, the soldier who got killed just before the Armistice, November the tenth, do you see what I mean? They wouldn't have punished you now, you would not have been so . . . in their hands.'

'I didn't mind.'

120

nowadays they either cure them or make them die rather slowly; she was at least spared all of that. And so was I. Her father and I were unable to live together after she died, we couldn't understand one another at all. Now she, my Peggy, she would have been forty-five in July. The eleventh.'

'I—'

'Now for heaven's sake don't say you're sorry, don't feel ashamed, please, that is not why I showed her to you, it was to, I don't know, make her real again for me, sometimes she is not, not now, when it was so long ago. I don't want you to regret the wrong thing.'

'What's it to you, anyway?' Sullen.

'What are you to anyone?' Crisp.

Janet looked down at the photograph again. She would have thrown it, had it been of anything else, but a kind of superstition made her gentle with it, and somehow also overflowed, preventing the rough words that came to mind, stopped her reaching out and giving Mrs Downely the little hard shove, that's all it would have taken, to knock her over backwards into her chair, mad interfering old bag—

She put it down on the table between them, and drew a long breath.

'I haven't got a photograph,' she said.

21

TONIGHT ANNIE HAD BROUGHT A BAG OF SATSUMAS and *Good Housekeeping*. She made a star shape out of satsuma peel, flattening it with the heel of her hand while she listened.

'Where is he now then?'

'At his place,' said Marion, sniffing, not tearfully but because she had caught a cold. So had Lewis. All that damp air, she thought, looking through a crumpled Kleenex for a usable stretch. She found one, and blew her nose noisily.

'Well, honestly,' said Annie, 'I don't know what to say.' Which was at least partly true, since the various exclamations of astonished and rapturous excitement that sprang to mind seemed hardly suitable.

'Did you, you know, talk to him?'

'Not till we were on the way home. And then it was a bit difficult, Lewis kept waking up and yelling, I didn't know he was starting this cold, you see, nothing worked, I just couldn't settle him.'

'So you couldn't really get anywhere?'

'Well he just said, he just said it was all over ages ago and nothing to do with me. And I said, had he ever, oh God—'

'—What, you mean, other men?'

'Yes, and he said no, only Mel, and that he didn't want to talk about it because it was none of my business. And he just sounded, well, reasonable. I sort of thought, he's right, what's it got to do with me, only I keep . . . trembling; I keep feeling all shaky, I mean I don't know what I feel, really.'

Shocked, thought Annie, and shocked by being shocked. 'You mean, you don't know why you feel so bad about it?'

'In a way. I suppose.'

'It was quite a big secret.'

'Was it? You see, I don't think so, I bet it's quite common, I mean I don't know, does anyone know?'

Annie shrugged. She took another satsuma out of the bag and turned it over and over in her fingertips.

'Actually the worst bit – I asked him how long it had lasted, and he said, four years, I mean four years!'

'Yes—'

'It's hardly a passing fancy, is it, there's marriages don't last that long. I don't know if that makes it better or worse.'

'Better, surely.'

'Why? I said, But you never had a girlfriend for that long, and he said, no he hadn't come to think of it!'

'How was he, then? I mean, was he upset you'd found out, or relieved, or angry, or what?'

'That's it, I just don't know. He didn't seem anything very much. He was calm. Oh did you? he says, Sorry about that.'

'What are you going to do then?'

'Oh, I don't know. You know things have been absolutely awful between us, ever since the baby was born really.'

'You've been under a lot of strain.'

'So's everybody, with a new baby.'

'I think he's more difficult than most.'

'Oh, he ate a whole banana, did I tell you?'

'Yes,' said Annie, smiling.

125

'You just wait, you wait till you've got one, then you'll see, oh, sorry—'

'Doesn't matter. He wrote to me actually. Silly sod.'

'What d'you mean?'

'Didn't really say anything. I don't know what he thought he was up to.'

'Keeping the lines open?'

Annie shook her head. The satsuma had grown quite warm in her hands, and a little squashy within.

'Ann? D'you fancy coming to stay with me for a bit?'

'What, here?'

'Yes.' Marion blew her nose again. 'Just for a little while. I'd feel sort of safer. I know it's daft. Would you, please?'

Annie thought for a moment. She thought of her own flat, and the charge nurse, who sometimes arrived in her thoughts at night and sneered at her for remembering him. There would surely be less room for him here. Too much noise, too much company.

'No, forget it, it was just a thought.'

'Actually,' said Annie, 'I was thinking how much I'd like to come, I really want to. I've been a bit lonely,' she added, to cheer Marion up. 'It'd be nice. So, yes, all right.'

'Ooh, Annie, that's great, thanks!' Marion's eyes filled; though as she rushed off to check the airing cupboard for clean sheets she was also aware of a tremendous anxiety. She stared at the blankets and rolled up sleeping bags without seeing them, saying aloud to herself, very softly, Don't tell her, don't tell her that, don't tell her.

Sheets, sheets.

But I'm sure to, I nearly did just now.

Too shameful, don't tell her for Christ's sake.

'I'll help you make it up, shall I?'

'Oh, hallo, yes, thanks, all right—'

The spare room was full of Benny's things.

'He usually sleeps here,' whispered Marion, 'because the baby keeps him awake, you know, if I take him into bed

126

with me to feed him; he went on and on about the slurping noises.'

They laughed, softly.

'Lewis'll wake you up all the time, you know. I mean he's only next door.'

'I don't care.'

I'm going to tell her, thought Marion, feeling for a moment as if she had just reached the top of the roller-coaster, and was poised before the sudden headlong swoop downwards. It had been so erotic, seeing them kiss. And ever since, imagining them together, trying not to, I can't keep Benny out of my mind, I want to touch him myself. I want him back. I want him. And what does that make me? Just in time she saw the way out, a much gentler slope, gentle in comparison anyway, though once it had looked practically vertical, funny how things could change so fast:

'Actually we haven't slept together at all,' she said, in a low mutter, her eyes rather wild. 'Not since Lewis.'

'Oh.' Annie sat down on the bed. 'Crumbs,' she added helplessly.

'I just didn't want to, you know I had this awful—'

'Yes, yes,' hissed Annie, trying to stave off anything obstetrical. Marion had spent quite long enough going into such details already, she felt, and some of them had kept Annie awake at night.

'And then it just seemed clear that he didn't want to either, well, he never tried very hard, he didn't seem that interested, and of course we were both so tired all the time and me so fat—'

'Oh, come on—'

'And it's gone on so long now it just seems out of the question, it would be embarrassing, we haven't talked about it, we've just sort of got on with things,' whispered Marion more calmly. Put that like, she thought, it didn't sound quite so bad. Possibly it wasn't at all bad anyway, perhaps it was perfectly natural, perhaps it was what people always

127

used to do in the old days before sex was supposed to be so flaming good for you.

'Haven't you, well, missed it? At all?'

Marion sat down too. 'Not really. No. Anyway, there's you know, what I told you, when you're breast-feeding, you get this, sort of, substitute. I mean I don't know if it's that or just because if you're absolutely whacked it's the last thing you think about anyway.'

'But it was all right to start with?'

'Oh, I don't know. I suppose so.'

'Marion!'

'I can hardly remember to be honest. It all seems such a long time ago. I mean, do you? Do you miss it?'

'It's a bit hard to tell,' said Annie anxiously. 'I miss his company. It's because he's not there that I keep—'

'What?'

'Oh, nothing.' Remembering a look, remembering her response to it, normal or abnormal, that was the question. Funny that no matter how much you prided yourself on individuality in everything else, appearance, the books you read, conversation, interior decor, that kind of thing, as far as sex went you longed for the norm, if only you could be sure what that was. 'I wish I knew what other people did. I mean, felt; watching them at it wouldn't be much use either, would it?'

'You don't get prizes.'

'Don't you?'

There was a pause, and then Annie said, ''Cos if it's for holding onto your man I suppose we both get the wooden spoon,' and for several minutes afterwards they were both helpless with laughter, bent over in silent giggles.

'Come on. Let's get this bed made.' Sighing, still sniggering now and then, they straightened the sheets and blankets and crept downstairs again.

'Want some toast?'

'Mm, thanks. You'll have to talk to him, properly.'

'I know.'

128

'Look. Tell you what. I'll babysit, shall I? You could go out together, neutral ground, you know, somewhere public, where you'll have to sort of—'

'—behave ourselves, yes. Yes, all right. Thanks. I'll call him.'

'Any time. I'm not busy. Did – what was that, did you hear that?'

'Yeah, it's probably Muff I'm afraid, I must have forgotten to put the brick on top of the dustbin, he's got a real thing about dustbins . . .'

Outside in the darkness, hidden behind a bush, Muff was still watching the unusual visitor, who did one or two things more and then roared away. Presently, when it was quite clear the man wasn't coming back, Muff made his stealthy way out from under cover, to nose amongst the treasures that he had left behind.

22

RUSSELL HAD HAD A TERRIBLE WEEK. ON SATURDAY
night, coming home from the pub, he had thought of
playing a little game on someone, but found no one to play
it with, went on turning hopefully down one dark street
after another, miles out of his way, until finally, more out
of boredom than anything else, he had fallen in behind a
quite elderly woman with a stick, who ought, thought
Russell, to have known better than to be out late at night
on her own in a fur coat. Asking to be mugged, she was.
And fur coats were disgusting anyway. Serve her right, a
little scare. But he couldn't work up much enthusiasm, and
when she peeked round, as they always did, to make sure,
and he caught a glimpse of her watery old eyes, he felt
suddenly disgusted, as if he were doing something perverse.
He moved to the right and speeded up to overtake her on
the pavement, but as he drew level something seemed to
spring out sideways and hit him very hard across the ribs,
and as he yelled with surprise and staggered back the mad
old bitch pushed heavily against him, knocking him completely off balance. Russell fell heavily over backwards,
banging his head hard on the pavement, and lay stunned
for a moment. Cold fur pressed against his face, pushing
itself into his mouth and nose. In a panic he struggled

clear, and stood up gasping, to see what looked like several big blokes pounding down the street towards him, and the old bag, dead probably, at his feet.

'Oy, you!' a yell, from one of the pounding blokes. Russell ran for it, managing a glimpse, as he turned the corner, of a little crowd gathering back there, and some public-spirited bastard still after him.

'I didn't do anything!' Russell shouted hoarsely as he ran. He passed a very bad night, what with his aching ribs and the shock and unfairness of it, and had several sickening tremors the next day, putting the news on; and broke out in a sweat over a vision of Vicki idly watching *Crimewatch UK*, 'Hey Russell, this sounds just like you, look he had the same jacket on too, look, Russell . . . Russell?'

By Monday morning he felt he must be in the clear, but he was very low. It had taken him some time to realise that the old woman must have hit him with her stick, that he was someone who'd been knocked flat by an old-age-pensioner. Anyone would laugh, hearing about it; he had to snigger himself now and then. Even so, it was terribly upsetting. He felt betrayed, as if all his life people had been telling him he was one thing, and old ladies another, and he'd trustingly believed them, and now look! It was enough to make you wonder what else they'd got wrong.

And on Monday afternoon, as he was jogging slowly round the park along the boating lake, trying to take his mind off things, an Alsatian dog had come running towards him, friskily, he thought at first, until he noticed the strange still way it was holding its head. It came straight at him and before he had time even to yell it had bitten him swiftly on the bottom, tearing the back of his track suit. He went on running, dancing round, shouting, while it leapt up at him, catching his forearm in its crocodile jaws, letting go to rear up and lunge for his face.

Eventually he had managed to get in a good kick at its ribs, and then another at its stomach, and it had turned and dashed away looking alert, as if it had suddenly thought

131

of something better to do. Russell, heaving, covered in saliva and toothmarks, had staggered to the nearest bench and collapsed, and was still rather shaky when he got home, and Vicky, seeing his trousers, had giggled. Of course it was true enough that she didn't know he'd lately been floored by an old woman with a walking stick but Russell was in no mood to appreciate this and had immediately lost his temper.

Well, what did she expect, he'd told her afterwards. No one laughs at me like that. If she thought she could get away with it she could bloody well think again.

So now she was being the tragedy queen, sighing over the sink and staring out of the windows, I can't go to work like this, she'd said, when honestly there was hardly a mark, Russell couldn't see anything, anyway. She had a lot less to complain about than he had, he'd had to wait ages in Casualty and the tetanus injection had made his arm swell up, and his ribs still ached a bit and his bum hurt all the time, sitting, standing, walking about. Barney's motor-bike was plain murder, potholes everywhere, sometimes you just didn't see them in time or couldn't help but wallop straight over them, he hadn't planned the dustbin lark but by the time she'd finally parked he was in such a fury from the pain that he'd simply had to relieve his feelings some-how, just knowing her address hadn't seemed enough.

On Tuesday and Wednesday, his days off, he'd felt too ill to turn up at the clinic, so he'd had to take a couple more days off sick from his NHS job to make up for them, and even with a bona fide note from his GP it wasn't going to look good, not quite so soon. He had consoled himself a little by dialling 999 and directing the fire brigade to Miss Grey's house, quite late at night, to be sure she was in when they came hammering on the door.

Which had given him a few cosy little laughs, but when he went back to official work on Saturday all hell had broken loose, piles of paperwork in the office, the ward clerk had been off sick as well and both the staff were from an agency, and both new, so neither of them knew where anything was and kept interrupting him as he fought his way through the notes and letters and computer printouts with infuriating requests for biros, or a different stethoscope, this one doesn't seem to work, sorry, or toilet paper, or knives and forks, maddening at any time but unendurable with this pain in his arse and his arm still throbbing.

Must have been a duff jab, he kept thinking, and that was a bit of a worry, perhaps it was going to give him tetanus rather than stop him getting it, and he had gone to the staff loos for another quick look beneath the elastoplast and found that idiot bastard Morris, how had he got in there in the first place when the door was meant to be kept locked? hanging from a twisted pair of someone's tights looped over the window hook, with his tongue sticking out and his face all purple. Russell had stood there for a second simply unable to believe it was happening to him, didn't the stupid sod know he'd had a Written Warning, what the fuck did he think he was playing at?

Panicking a little, Russell had limped back to his office, scrabbled wildly amongst the papers, and eventually found a pair of scissors, and carrying these and a chair he had hurried back to the loos, shouting for help. But in the heat of the moment he couldn't remember the names of either of the agency nurses, and one of them had gone on her lunch break anyway, and the other one, finally located playing Scrabble in the day room, had rushed off to call the crash team and then had to rush back again, because she didn't know what the code was. He'd had a moment's pleasure telling her what he thought of her for that.

As chance would have it Morris was already coughing and cursing by the time they all came thundering in, Okay, he'd said, panic over, but there it was, a near miss, nothing like as good as a mile, so Miss Grey would say, when she read the report, as she no doubt would.

As if it was his fault – how can I spend time nattering to patients, ear to the ground sort of thing, when I've got all this sodding paperwork to go through, they're lucky I turned up at all, I should've taken the whole week off, I would've done if it wasn't for Her.

Well, she was asking for it now.

I know where you live, thought Russell, riding Barney's motorbike slowly home. He went over all the reasons he had to be angry, the impossible job he'd somehow been misled into and was now fairly stuck with, Vicki moping, his sore arse and bruised ribs and the whole world playing sly tricks on him whenever it chose.

Well it was all a bit much. You had to fight back, thought Russell, steering carefully round another pothole, spotted just in time. You had to fight back or go under.

I know where you live, and the next time I come to call you're going to know all about it.

23

PETER PUT THE RECEIVER DOWN. SHE WAS STILL out, then. He went back to his typewriter, where Chapter Seven, the longer by one sluggish line, made his spine flex and his fingers go stiff; his very bones, he thought, could no longer endure the boredom, his body simply would not allow itself to be propped in front of Chapter Seven for so much as one minute more.

He got up and went to the kitchen, where several cans of beer beckoned. The sound of relief, as one hissed itself open in his hand! Like a sigh.

Perhaps she'd gone on holiday, he thought. On her own, or with another girl. The thought of her packing her suitcase all by herself filled him with tenderness, for he was troubled constantly at present by the idea of Annie going to work or doing her shopping, doing perfectly ordinary things but somehow doing them bravely, on her own. The fairly frequent picture of her getting on her little motorbike in her absurd Evel Knievel outfit and buzzing along at ten miles an hour in her goggles sometimes made his throat ache and his eyes water; he seemed unable to control this curious tendency to see her as waif-like and courageous, and it was dreadfully irritating, catching himself at it once again.

So what if she'd gone on holiday!

He saw her sitting at a table in the sun, being eyed by some brainless hunk in a vest; and then remembered her laughing over a body-building magazine in Smith's, Look, they've got trilobites stuck on their chests! and laughed himself, as if with her.

You will never replace me, she said immediately, while the cold wind blew her hair across her eyes.

Shut up.

Peter took the beer into his sitting room and put the television on. A couple in bed, all naked heaving shoulders, BBC1; Americans sobbing over a hospital bed, BBC2; gardening on ITV and a nice picture of a rainbow on the new Channel Four, still clearly having trouble with advertising: gardening, then, thought Peter, gloomily switching back.

'And within twelve hours there were dragon-flies over the water—'

A man with a beard and wellingtons stood bowed beside a muddy pond, laying squares of turf like limp hairy carpet tiles.

'And this gentle slope, you see, encourages all sorts of wildlife, makes it accessible—' Yearning swoopy music accompanied a sudden shot of buttercups blowing in the breeze. It was, thought Peter, the sort of garden his father would take all sorts of strong measures with, Tumbleweed, Slugdeath, Flitgun, for the old boy tended toward the municipal, inserting orderly alternate blue lobelia and white alyssum to edge his daisy-free lawn, and lurid petunias, and primulas in rows; only his vegetable patch was beautiful, and that was by accident; order there was beautiful. Whereas flowers need a little disorder, thought Peter, and dad will never understand that in a million years; he wouldn't want a wildlife garden if it was stocked with blue fritillaries and a unicorn, he likes a neat lawn and tidy beds, he is anti-Life, thought Peter, getting quite worked up. He opened another can and swigged it grimly through its hole.

136

I'd have a wildlife garden, I'd have accessible water and frog-spawn, I'd have toads clasped in plexus in the rockery and nettles for the butterflies.

If I had a garden.

She'd like a wildlife garden too.

You will never replace me, said Annie, pulling the hair away from her eyes.

Suppose it was true? Look at old Joe after all. He'd stopped trying long ago. He would've been all right if Annabel had lived, she'd've gone off with someone else soon enough, she'd never have married him the way he had irrevocably married himself to her once she had died. All because Joe hadn't taken her a cup of tea. If he'd taken in the tea the way he usually did she'd still be alive probably and Joe would have been someone else, he might have married someone, had children, people did; and if Joe had done that I would have too, probably. But he's stuck where he was, and so am I, stuck with him.

Wonder if he knows.

Annabel! Undress quietly, slide in beside her, pounce surprise!

Peter opened his eyes cautiously, and sat still for a moment, watching the man with the beard and wellingtons wading in the water, but this time there was no getting away from that blue rictus or the lacy froth of her blood, the bed soaked, soiled, his own roaring scream had terrified him, he had scrabbled himself out and away trying to cover himself, he had run into the door and hurt his shoulder, and the telephone was ringing and ringing, he had fallen down the stairs, actually fallen rolling all the way down them, leaping up at the bottom as careless as an animal, reached the hallway, vomited without effort or direction and picked up the receiver, his hand had reached out all by itself, and his voice had said, only panting a little:

'Hallo?'

'Pete? Joe. Is Annabel there, because she's missed a

morning lecture apparently and we were supposed to meet for lunch. Is she there?'

A blank.

'I don't know.'

'Well, either she's there or she isn't,' said Joe. 'Can you go and check, she might even be asleep still, I didn't wake her up, see. Just give her a shout.'

'Oh. All right then.'

'I'll hang on.'

Peter could not answer. He put the phone down carefully, so as not to hurt Joe's ear with any sudden clunking noises, and went back up stairs. The door as in a nightmare stood ajar, the little pile of Peter's clothes holding it open. And there she was, still dead.

He had grabbed the clothes and run back into his own room, suddenly trembling too much to do the buttons up, quick just a sweater then, but in control again, so that the various parts of himself that he had bruised in the fall downstairs began to hurt quite badly. He had limped back down hanging onto the banisters, for, as it would turn out, he had sprained his ankle and cracked a bone in his elbow.

'Hallo?' Thinking fast now. 'Joe? Look, I think you better come round straight away, I think Annabel's ill, can you come now?'

'What is it, is she, I'm coming—'

And then the ambulance, and a nice policewoman had made him a cup of tea, and someone had come in from next door and mopped up where he had been sick, and Joe had arrived just as they were getting her down the stairs, they were being very careful, Joe shouting *What, what's happening, what's going on?*

Known epileptic, her bracelet, the drugs beside the bed.

'Did you know her, sir?'

'She's my girlfriend, what's happening? Annabel, Annabel!'

And him working it out: if I'd woken her up she would have taken her pills, but I let her sleep and she died. How

138

long had it taken her? an hour, perhaps, longer, had she woken up and realised? she didn't get much of an aura, sometimes, she said, she could smell honey, then she knew, had she woken and felt terror? had she been aware while she died, what was I doing? taking notes in Lab 28 all morning while she died, I let her sleep. I killed her.

Seeing him working it out.

'You found her, did you sir?'

'Yes. I found her.'

'Is she dead? Is she?'

'You sit down, sir, you take it easy—'

Very nice they were, the ambulanceman, the police, all so gentle, well, thought Peter now, I suppose we were all so young, we must have seemed like children to them. She'd just turned nineteen. I loved her. I was ashamed of her, taking me to bed when she was shacked up with Joe, what a bitch, I thought then, what a sly heartless tart. And me, what a bastard! But she was only nineteen. She was only playing. She was lovely, and I loved her, and so did Joe.

Peter, by now quite drunk, brushed the tears from his eyes.

My dad was right, my old dad. Of course it happened to me. As well. I wish I'd told Joe I was fucking her, but how can I now? She was fucking me, she was always in charge. But she was only playing.

He got up, and staggered a little. Time for bed. Oh Annie my Annabel!

Not to undress. Pounce surprise. Face down across his bed Peter fell asleep, and soon began to dream.

He went to visit Stanley, with Annie. Stanley was very pleased to see them.

'Come round the back,' he said, 'I've got something to show you,' and they followed him round the house, but instead of his usual tiny municipal back garden there was a great park, a huge landscaped masterpiece, with lots of

139

trees in blossom and flowers everywhere, and butterflies, and a great wood, with distant views beyond it, of the sea.

'Look!'

'It's . . . fantastic!'

'Come and see the pond; your mother's putting the turf down.'

'Hallo Mum!'

'Hallo love. What d'you think of it then?'

'I can't believe it, it's beautiful, has it really been here all the time?'

They nodded, their arms round each other.

'But why didn't you tell me?'

'Look, Peter!'

From the corner of his eye he saw a clean young fox rise from its afternoon lazing, and trot away into the bushes.

He began to feel angry. All these years he'd lived here and they'd kept this wonderful garden a secret!

'Why didn't you tell me?' he asked again, and Stanley looked slightly embarrassed, and said that they hadn't been able to tell him, because if he had known about it he would have used it, to bring women to, to seduce them. 'So we couldn't, could we?'

Peter felt furiously resentful, and at the same time ashamed, for he knew that it was true, and that he would have done so.

'But we can come now,' said Annie. 'Did you see the fox?'

Peter woke up. He felt cold and greasy and hungry and sick. In the bathroom he remembered the dream, and sniggered a little; it seemed so transparent. Surely your unconscious was supposed to dress things up a bit more than that? Perhaps it reckons I'm too thick for anything more subtle, he thought, and perhaps it's got a point.

She might not want me back by now, he told it, as he ran a bath, but all the same he felt quite cheerful. Wish I hadn't sent that letter, or been so angry when I wrote it.

140

But she was sure to overlook it, once he had explained. Surely.

Them and their garden. I hope it was true. The garden of sexual happiness, of marital delights. Presumably. Old Stanley. Could it be true? He thought of them embracing, caught now and then in the kitchen, his father touching his mother's cheek.

Well, what do I know about anything?

The water was hot. He got in, and lay back, groaning.

24

NO LIGHT WAS VISIBLE ROUND THE DOOR. JANET rang the bell again, and considered trying to peer in through the letter-box, but as she reached down to see how stiff it was she heard a faint sound from within, the click of an inner door opening. Bolts scraped, and the door opened a fraction.

'Who is it please?' Rather quavery.

'Mrs Downely? Erm, it's me. Janet McIver.' The chain rattled, and the door opened.

'Oh, hallo dear—'

Terrible colour, really pasty, and had she looked a bit blank there for a moment, before the smile? Though the smile made her look exactly herself again. 'Hallo!' Janet fluttered in the doorway. 'I was worried about you, I was waiting and waiting, when you were late, and then you didn't come, and I thought—'

'Come in.'

Mrs Downely wore a maroon padded dressing gown. She looked very small without her heels on, Janet thought, following her into the front room. She felt a tremendous elation. All alone she had worked out that Mrs Downely might be ill, she had come to the right block of flats and climbed the stairs to the right floor and rung the bell. And here she was, seeing Mrs Downely, doing what she wanted to do instead of just thinking about it and deciding it was all too risky and going home to argue miserably with herself all night.

'I bet you never thought I'd come to see you!' she said, and Mrs Downely, who had been hoping to get back to bed as soon as possible, heard the pride in her voice, and felt, for a moment, at a loss.

Whatever am I to do with her? she wondered. 'It's very nice of you,' she said.

Janet meanwhile had noticed certain signs of disarray, the hearth full of ashes, a teacup on the mantelpiece, the curtain not quite straight. She hesitated. 'I wondered if you were ill,' she said at last.

'Just a little tired.'

'Oh, shall I go, I don't want to—'

'No, not just yet, please. I wonder if you would mind making us some tea—'

'Oh right—' Leaping up. Charging off. Well, well, thought Mrs Downely, this is rather a surprise. Though possibly not, if you thought about it. I suppose all she ever wanted was a little attention.

She yawned extensively, and closed her eyes.

'Mrs Downely?'

Janet set the tray on the small gnarled table by the fireplace. She sat down very slowly so as not to make any noise, and leant forward, studying Mrs Downely's face. All week she had been longing to be back here; it was like being in love. I just wanted to see her, thought Janet, a little surprised; for earlier, on tenterhooks at rehearsal, when Mrs Downely didn't come and didn't come, she had been thinking that all she wanted was to listen, to hear Mrs Downely say again, preferably, what she had said last time, but without the initial shock of it, so she could listen properly and think about it, not muddle it up with her own reactions.

But now she was actually here it was pleasant just to

143

look, and try to get her face off by heart. I wish she were something to do with me, thought Janet, I wish she was an aunt or something, then she wouldn't be able to get rid of me.

'Hallo.' Janet smiled.

'Have I been asleep? How awful, I'm so sorry—'

'Would you like something to eat, some toast or something?'

'No, no thank you, just tea, please.'

There was a small stain of egg yolk on the front of the dressing gown, Janet noticed.

'What's wrong? Won't you tell me?'

'Don't get all dramatic, please. Really, I am just tired. I haven't been sleeping. Oh, it's so boring – I got mugged. It's rather upset me, so I can't sleep.'

'What happened?'

'Well. I was walking home, from a friend's. I always do, it's no distance. It was a little later than usual, that's all. And I realised someone was following me. A man. And I know you're supposed to just hand everything over, I intended to, I'd thought about it, I had hardly any money on me anyway, just a bag I was rather fond of, I thought, oh well, it's only a bag; but as he came up close, I don't know, I just couldn't do it, I felt so *cross*. I thought, why should I just hand over my perfectly nice bag to this stranger merely because he demands it? And I hit him instead. With my stick.' Mrs Downely giggled. 'Which was a very silly thing to do, because of course I need the stick to balance with, and as soon as I bashed him I fell over, it must have looked extremely comical. I knocked him over as well.'

'What happened, did he—'

'He just ran off. There was a crowd all of a sudden, someone even chased after him I think, oh and the police were called, and an ambulance, it was the most awful fuss, and everyone was clearly highly entertained and jolly pleased with me, you know, battling granny kind of thing.

144

Frightful. And I was perfectly all right, well actually simply tremendous bruises all down one side, real purple Hammer Horror stuff but nothing that really hurts, rather curious, but I kept on remembering how he'd shouted when I hit him, he shouted "Ow, stop it, stop it!" and he sounded so aggrieved and frightened, like a child. I was ashamed. And upset, and I still am and I'm not at all sure with whom, or with whom the most, if that makes sense. That's all.'

'It was his own fault,' said Janet after a pause.

'No,' said Mrs Downely sadly. 'He was horrible and I was horrible back. I suppose there is a case for saying he started it but only a playground one. I must say I hadn't realised before that there is another reason for turning the other cheek. That you actually feel better afterwards, I mean.'

'You might not have. You don't know, do you. You might have been lying awake feeling really cross with yourself for letting him get away with it. You don't take sugar, do you?'

'No, thank you. You're right, I would have been cross. But I wouldn't have lost sleep over it. I've never hit anyone before. I've frightened myself, when I thought I have nothing further to be afraid of. Still. I'll get over it, let's not talk about it anymore. How did rehearsal go?'

'Oh!' Janet jumped a little in her chair, rattling her teacup. 'There's a letter for you. We all had one. Mr Laidlaw was standing by the door handing them out. It's about the conductor.' She rifled through her handbag and produced an envelope. 'Here.'

'Won't you tell me? No glasses—'

'Yes, he says the committee's decided to chuck him, Robert I mean, because he's too expensive, they're not renewing his contract. Next season.'

'Oh dear.' Mrs Downely opened the letter, held it at arm's length, and squinted at it. 'Oh dear. ". . . very much regret . . . blah blah . . . current financial situation blah

145

blah blah . . . suggestions from the floor". Well well well. How was this document received, would you say?'

'Erm—' Janet hesitated. She had not taken very much notice at the time, she had been too worried about Mrs Downely not showing up. She thought back. 'Erm, I don't know. There was a bit of muttering I suppose. I heard someone saying his timing was a bit off. Mr Laidlaw's. And it was embarrassing when he came in, the conductor. There was a sort of funny silence. I think.'

'What about the interval, what were people saying then?'

Janet thought. She had spent the time searching through the register, finding 'Apols' written against Mrs Downely's name, enquiring boldly, she felt, from a woman who happened to be standing next to her what this could mean, and then wondering dolefully over the world of manners and etiquette and why it was she knew so little about it. 'Oh, someone made a speech,' she said, suddenly remembering. 'Said it was such a big decision we ought to have a . . . special meeting—'

'An EGM? Extraordinary General Meeting? When?'

'Before next week's rehearsal. At seven, and the rehearsal's not to start till eight. It was all proposed and seconded.'

'Sounds very serious.'

'Oh and first, this old guy Albert, you know on the committee, he stands up and says "Point of order, the committee's decision is actually final," and honestly there was a sort of roar—'

'No!'

'Yes, and this woman with glasses, that had made the speech—'

'Mrs Lauderdale, no doubt—'

'Dunno, she says "No, this is a democracy, we ought to get a vote on it," and there was a sort of cheer, really, and laughing, then it was all deciding when to do it, have the special meeting and that. Then Robert comes back in and everyone's all shuffling and coughing, I mean I don't know if he's in on it all or not, I suppose he must be—'

146

'Oh, what a pity I missed it! It sounds such fun. I thing Stanley may have a revolution on his hands.'

'What, Mr Laidlaw?'

'Well, I'm not certain of course. But I think Stanley has made a big mistake. He hasn't noticed how much the choir has changed. It is one of the many things that has become more middle-class. It is full of people striving after Art. Not singing for fun, as it was years ago. And Robert is part of all that. He may be unpleasantly high-handed and distant and always rushing off back to Bromley, apparently he can only just catch the last train, had you heard that? But he's good, you see, and he's making us better, and if we have to choose between him and Stanley, Art or fun, I rather think Stanley's for the high jump, don't you?'

'But if it's financial—'

'It's not entirely financial. It's more to do with power. Who's in charge, Stanley and the general committee, or our hired conductor? Stanley is Treasurer, you see. Being in charge of the money always makes people think they're in charge of everything else.'

'But if we really can't afford him—'

'We will vote to put up the fees. That's my bet. We will have to pay more to sing. And it's tumbrils and the guillotine for Stanley and the general committee; I'm rather looking forward to it, nothing personal of course.'

'You'll be going then?'

'Of course. I feel much better already. I'm so pleased you came, you've cheered me up immensely. Taken my mind off things, you see.'

'Good,' said Janet, shyly.

'The last rehearsal's going to be rather a trial, isn't it. Though of course there is actually a proper run through with the orchestra on the Saturday afternoon.'

'I might have to miss that. I'm working.'

'Oh don't. Can't you swop, or something? Really it's essential. You won't know where you're sitting or anything. I put you down to sit next to me, is that all right? But you mustn't miss it. It's such a thrill, when the orchestra first begins, and we sound so real. And if you miss seeing the hall when it's empty you won't feel properly awed and terrified when it's full.'

'Will it be full? I'd never heard of the piece. I wouldn't have come.'

'No, but for a musical middlebrow you are extraordinarily ignorant. Believe me, it may be slightly on the modern side but it's very popular, all those crashes and jumps, there won't be a spare seat. And as well as the Mendelssohn anthem the orchestra will be doing a nice piece of Elgar before the interval. We'll have a full house. It'll be next year's Bach that keeps them away in droves.'

Mrs Downely sighed, and put her cup down. 'Whereas this, it's such a successful piece, I mean that it makes you feel the emotions it contains. The way a successful thriller makes your heart pound; you're in no danger yourself, are you, sitting there in the dark with a choc-ice, but your physical self behaves as if it were. And we will be up there on the stage, no I mean down, it's the Festival Hall of course, down there on the stage feeling all these powerful emotions, and with a far less vicarious thrill, because we are making the sound that produces the effect, we are our own audience. But without any of the real exposure that comes from, say dramatic acting, on a stage. Safe exhibitionism, that's what it is. A real tonic for repression, no wonder it's so popular.'

'Even if we don't have the melody line,' said Janet.

'What? Oh, you mean you and I, well, so few of us do. Only the sopranos really. Doesn't matter, does it, only the overall sound matters.'

Janet nodded. Right back to normal, she was thinking. Because I came to see her. 'I should be going,' she said eventually. Don't stay too long. Don't spoil it.

'Wait a minute. Please. There was something in particular I wanted to say to you. I've been thinking about you, quite a lot,' Mrs Downely added, rather apologetically.

'Oh?' Janet smiled nervously.

'Yes. All that lying awake at night, you see. I thought about you and your, difficulties. Among other things.'

Janet stopped smiling.

'What?' she said unwillingly. It sounded as if she was going to hear something new, and she wasn't sure she wanted to, just yet.

'Well, I thought that so much of your pain comes from passivity. There being nothing you can do. You just have to sit there. Like being in the audience. So I thought, suppose you could write to him.'

'What?'

Rather to her surprise Mrs Downely found herself beginning to tremble. Janet looked blank, not even questioning. I might just make things worse, thought Mrs Downely in fright.

'Write to him, I don't mean directly, I mean to whatever authority arranged the adoption. He must have a file somewhere – they are required to keep all that sort of thing. You could write to him, care of the authority,' said Mrs Downely, beginning to speak very quickly. 'They could keep the letters for you. Or if they refuse you could keep them yourself. Anyway if he ever decides to find you, and he might well – not soon; it seems to me that people tend to be well into their twenties before they begin to care a great deal about blood ties, that sort of thing, especially if he has been happy with his adopted parents – well if and when he tries to find you there will be a pile of letters written over the years. It will be a demonstration of something. Every year, on his birthday, something like that, I thought, it will prove to him that whatever you did you have never forgotten him or carried on regardless or in fact hardly had a single day when you didn't wish and wish—'

Mrs Downely stopped suddenly, breathing very loudly through her nose. 'Well think about it anyway,' she said abruptly.

There was a short silence.

'I will,' said Janet after it. 'I will think about it.' Though already she saw the pile of yellowing letters in her mind, waiting somewhere for the grown-up stranger. Better than nothing, surely. Better than silence. Hardly the music, hardly the melody line, but better than nothing.

Mrs Downely was blowing her nose.

'Viola?'

'Yes?'

'I was wondering – will you play me next season's Bach?'

25

MARION, ARRIVING ON TIME, WALKED ROUND THE block so as to be a little late, and bought a newspaper on the way in case he was later still. But once inside she saw him straight away.

'Benny.'

'Hallo. Um, I got you a white wine, is that all right?'

'Lovely, thanks.' She sat down, trembling with nerves.

'You look very nice,' said Benny immediately. 'Is that new?'

Marion blushed. 'Annie talked me into it,' she said, lest Benny assume that looking her best to meet him meant anything. She wanted him hopeless for a while yet. Or possibly for good. It all depends, she thought vaguely. I don't know what on. On something.

'Good for Annie, it's nice, you look lovely.'

'Thank you.' He was looking well himself, in a neat dark suit, thinner than usual, which was always a good sign with him; he feels released, she thought. He wants us to be friends, probably. How will that feel, when he says that?

'How's it going?' she asked, carefully neutral.

'Oh, pretty well, you know, just getting started. How's Lewis?'

'Snotty,' said Marion. 'But not feverish or anything. Fine really.'

'Annie be all right, d'you think?'

'I told her where we'd be going, I told her to call, you know, if anything—'

'Right, right. Good.' There was a long silence.

'How about you, you all right?' he said. Marion looked down at the table. She thought that anyone who so much as glanced at them must instantly realise why they were sitting here like this.

Splitting up. She remembered a couple she had sat near once, in a restaurant, who had talked occasionally in low careful voices, but with the unmistakable rhythms of reproach, and whose eyes she had most anxiously avoided, lest they realise how obvious their situation was to anyone within yards of them.

Come on, get it over with, get started anyway. She sighed.

'What do you think?' she said.

She had heard something, she thought, as soon as she came in, but, since the room was so clearly empty, had dismissed and forgotten it. But there it was again, sure enough. What the hell was it?

Janet got up, turned the television sound down, and sat still for nearly a minute. A car went by, a front door opened somewhere down the street and closed again. Otherwise, nothing. Janet straightened up, and as she did so the noise instantly repeated itself: a muffled scrabbling sound.

She held her breath. Where was it coming from? It sounded so close. There, again. The little hairs on her arms and legs rose upright. Janet turned, and made a sudden hopping movement back into her armchair, where she knelt, breathing fast. Something, some creature, was trapped somewhere. In the walls somehow. What, though? A mouse? Could a mouse make so hefty a scratching sound?

A rat, thought Janet, it must be a rat caught there, Oh God and I heard it yesterday as well, I thought it was

152

Muff, I heard it scratching, how long has it been there? It must be stuck, it'll die, it'll starve, I'll have to listen to it scrabbling, a rat, starving, there it goes again, oh God—

Behind the gas fire. It was definitely behind the gas fire. Slowly Janet uncurled her legs and crept up to it, and peered beneath. All blocked off. No way out there.

If it's behind the fire I can get it out.

A rat, though! She saw herself levering the thing away from the wall, and the desperate animal, big as a cat, flinging itself, all bloodied claws and fangs, into her face, or running horribly round her room, it would skate about like a great furry spider.

I can't do it. I can't do that.

The scrabble sounded again.

Stuck down there in the dark, taking ages to die.

'Oh Jesus,' whimpered Janet.

Two flights down Annie and Lewis were watching the nine o'clock news. Lewis had removed his socks, and was placidly sucking one of them; the other he had lodged deep into the loading mechanism of the video recorder, but Annie had no suspicion of this as yet, and felt that on the whole things were going very well, that Marion's trouble was trying to play Lewis by the rules, making him go to bed at set times and eat regularly and so forth when it was obviously far less trouble all round to let him do what he wanted while he was too small to do anything very much.

'When are you going to get some teeth, then, eh?'

Very jolly, his smile. It was a lot like having a puppy around, Annie thought, a small friendly speechless creature amusing itself at your feet. Except that once or twice now, when he'd been looking at her sideways, he'd briefly worn her own mother's face, familiar from the album; her mother's baby face, apart from Benny's eyebrows. This was the sort of baby my grandmother looked after, Annie had thought. She would recognise him.

153

'Don't know what you'd think of her, though,' said Annie, bending down to tickle Lewis's toes, 'right old besom she was.'

Russell climbed gingerly onto Barney's motorbike, and wobbled into the middle of the road. He had loitering in mind, with, possibly, a certain intent, if the coast turned out to be clear. A swathe of broken glass on the front path, perhaps, or maybe just the dustbin again if all the lights were on. Depends what I feel when I get there, he told himself. But if the lights are off—

If the lights are off I ring the bell. If there's no answer, that's it. I get in. If I feel like it.

It would be perfectly simple. Only women there, and never bothering with the mortice lock, he'd seen all of them now, the one with the baby, the other one, and her, all of them just slamming the door behind them, silly girls. Just locked it properly at night, probably. Didn't they know how easy it was to slide a Yale lock open? All you needed was a nice slim sheet of bendy steel, like this, thought Russell, pressing the pocket of his jacket with one elbow, slide it between the door and the jamb and you were in, no sound, nothing broken, and any nosy neighbour or passer-by would think the door had been opened from the inside.

And then you were in. If you felt like it. If you just wanted to know what it would feel like to get in you could leave it at that, maybe leave just a little something, some sign, to let her know you'd been to call, or that someone had, someone who wished her ill. Just to let her know she's not safe. That I could do what I wanted. If I felt like it.

She's not to know I'm only playing, is she? Russell gave a little laugh at that, at her being so frightened all for nothing. That was the best part of it, really, he thought.

*

Peter decided to walk, there was no hurry, and he could stop on the way, he thought, and get her something, Annie always did, some flowers perhaps. And even if she wouldn't tell him what Annie was up to or where she was she would surely pass on the letter.

It's just asking her to meet me, he would say, I just want to see her, that's all.

And when I see her I will tell her about that dream. She'll love that. That'll clinch it. It was you, Annie, I could only get into the garden with you.

And I'll tell her about Annabel, properly, because I've never told anyone what really happened and I'll tell her that too. And she will tell me what it means. Her gloves, her handbag, she was right about that, she made sense about that. She will make sense of Annabel. Because I can't.

All these years I'd thought I'd almost forgotten her, but it isn't so, she's always been there, and I hadn't noticed, I don't think I noticed anyway.

I hadn't even noticed their names, Annie, Annabel. It is a question, thought Peter, walking quickly, of a certain frame of mind. One I have avoided getting into. Like mum and dad, that time I was ill.

I could tell her that, too.

Once when I was a kid, thought Peter, telling Annie, my mother met the Lord Mayor, who shook her hand while the cameras flashed, why I can't remember, I only remember the great family row afterwards:

For as Amy returned in triumph to her place, Stanley, it was alleged, had said nothing pleasant or congratulatory, hadn't so much as smiled, had just leant forward without even bothering to lower his voice and told his wife that the label at the back of her dress had been sticking up for all to see.

Amy's mother, mysteriously also present, had taken great offence at this, seeing her daughter's face. She too had leant forward, and angrily told Stanley what she thought of him, at some length. Accounts of what happened next had varied. Amy's mother claimed that Stanley, mottled as a turkey, had uttered gross insults; she had detailed these on request, to Peter's mingled horror and delight.

'Daddy, what does bleeder mean?'

Stanley, less forthcoming, had merely laid down the evening paper and slapped Peter's cheek. Peter had been very surprised; he had judged the word to be only bad enough to tease and annoy his father, not enrage him. He had gone howling to his mother, who had been peeling potatoes over the sink, scratching out their eyes with a fierce twist of the peeler. She had at first been less than sympathetic, had briskly dried his eyes on the tea-towel without a word, but then, perplexingly, she had reached up and taken a small bar of chocolate from the top shelf of the larder, and given it to him, adding only that Peter's father and his Nanna were a right pair, and that as far as she herself was concerned they could both of them take a running jump.

The entrancing image of them doing so, scowling but hand in hand, remained in Peter's mind for many years afterwards – he could see it now – while the immediate effect of the row was to keep him awake at night, and consequently very dozy and abstracted at school by day.

Presently he began to feel sick in the mornings, and prone to put his head down on his desk. His teacher threw bits of chalk at him and took to creeping up behind him and playfully hitting him very hard over the head with an exercise book, but still Peter's mother went on plonking Stanley's breakfast down in front of him and stalking in silence back to the kitchen, while the Sugar Smacks turned to ashes in Peter's mouth.

Eventually, summoned to the headmaster's study and accused outright of idleness and malingering Peter had, in what seemed to him an amazing piece of good luck, felt immediately so much worse that he had had to rush choking from the room, and had only just made it to the cloakroom in time.

Soon after that the row came mysteriously to an end. Nanna was allowed in the house again, his mother sipped her tea at the table with his dad. The tonic from the doctor stained Peter's teeth pale green and gave him further stomach upsets and bouts of constipation but apart from these minor difficulties he was perfectly well again.

But no one said anything, d'you see, Annie? No one connected me being ill with the row. I didn't either, I've only just thought of it, I've only just remembered all this. And I really was anaemic, and the tonic really made me better.

So what does that mean? Being ill worked – all that talk of pallor and listlessness scared the St Michael's label right back into place – but how did I do it? Did I do it? Did some part of my brain come up with anaemia, there, that'll show them, that'll get them talking again? All the rest of me was just having a bit of trouble getting to sleep at night. What told my spleen to act up?

And I'm remembering this now because of Annabel, whom I hadn't thought I'd thought of for years, Annabel who'd been in so many beds just before I climbed into them, everyone's, perhaps even yours, Annie. How am I to know?

Please be in, thought Peter at Marion as he waited at a zebra crossing. Please be in, and let me in too.

Janet, hesitating on the landing, thought that she could smell gas, and went to check her own stove in the kitchen, but everything was OFF there. She came out again, and sniffed. Definitely something. Was it gas?

She went slowly down the stairs, sniffing hard, but by the time she reached the ground floor could smell only Dettol. Marion had clearly just had to mop up again. Still, thought Janet, I'd better mention it, the gas, just in case, the baby might have been playing with the knobs or something. Come on. Knock. She's got to do something. She is the landlady after all. If there's rats she's got to do something about it—

Using this resentment as courage Janet rapped on Marion's front room door.

'Oh!' The woman who opened it looked startled, even, for a moment, rather scared.

'Oh,' said Janet, also taken by surprise. 'I'm—' she pointed ' – upstairs, I—'

'Oh, yes, of course, sorry, I didn't recognise you, come in, please.'

The woman stepped back. Behind her Janet saw the baby, bug-eyed on the floor, toys everywhere, and the television on; it looked very cosy.

'I'm baby-sitting, I'm Annie, I'm Marion's sister.'

'Janet, hallo.'

Doesn't look a bit like Felicity, Annie was thinking indignantly. Marion had said she was the image of her, what could she have been thinking of? God I thought she'd broken in for a moment, she saw herself telling Marion later, hadn't a clue who she was.

'What can I do for you?'

'There's something, there's something wrong with my gas fire. Upstairs. I think there's something stuck behind it.'

'Well. I'm sorry. Only it's nothing to do with me, you see, I'm only staying here for a bit, Marion'll be back soon, I could pass on a message, shall I?'

'I – hallo,' said Janet to Lewis, who had pulled himself to his feet by grasping the edge of her skirt and hauling on it, 'Hallo, you. How are you?'

'He's furious,' said Annie, smiling. 'Didn't you hear him? He wants Postman Pat I think, anyway I can't get the video to work, he's very annoyed about it. Aren't you?'

'How old is he?'

158

'Nearly a year. Isn't he awful, he must wake you up all the time.'

'No. I never hear him. I've hardly seen him actually. He's lovely.'

'Yes. Well, I'm sorry about the gas fire—'

'No, look, there's something behind it that's alive. It's got stuck. I can hear it, you see, scratching, I've tried to move it, but it's too heavy, I just need a hand, if we could shift it away from the wall a bit whatever it is can get out.'

'Oh. What is it, though?'

'I don't know. Well. I suppose it might be a mouse.'

'That sodding Muff,' said Annie, 'that bloody cat, you'd think it'd be some use.'

At this something turned in Janet's mind, a hint of Dettol, a whiff of gas, but she was too taken up with not mentioning rats to look at it properly.

'Have you got a torch?' she asked. 'Because if I had a torch I could find out what it is for sure down there.'

'Oh, torch, well, I don't live here, let me think, I'm sure she's got one somewhere, just a sec—'

As Janet had half suspected, finding the torch somehow committed Annie to coming upstairs with her to help with the fire.

'You don't mind if I bring Lewis, do you?'

'Of course not, hope he doesn't—'

They climbed the stairs, and Janet remembered what she had wanted to say earlier.

'Can you smell gas?'

Annie sniffed. 'No. But I've got a bit of a cold. Can you?'

'I thought I could earlier, I thought the baby might have fiddled with the knobs or something, I meant to mention it.'

Annie shook her head. 'We haven't been in the kitchen actually. I could go and check, shall I nip down now, is it strong?'

'No. I can hardly smell it now, just the Dettol really.'

159

'Yeah, Muff strikes again, you've got a lot to put up with in this house.'

'In here,' said Janet, 'come in.'

'Oh, right,' said Annie, disconcerted again, for she had been expecting a roomful of Felicity, lots of complicated curtains and appliqué-work cushions and little lamps everywhere, and instead the place was practically unfurnished, she thought, and rather restful, actually, after the toy-strewn mess downstairs. She put Lewis down on the plain blue rug with his bottle. The stillness and airiness of the room made Annie feel a little shy, she imagined Janet looking round her own flat back in Hackney and sneering at the knick-knacks, I'm definitely getting rid of those soppy sea shells, thought Annie, soon as I get home they're out.

'So, it's behind here, is it, whatever it is?'

As Janet nodded the sound came again, a sudden quite loud scrabbling. Both of them jumped.

'Crumbs. What the hell is it?'

Janet shrugged. 'Dunno. But I can't just leave it there, can I?'

'Bit creepy, isn't it?'

The sound came again, a long volley of scratches and thuds.

'What's it doing?' whispered Annie over the noise, which went on and on, contained and frantic. Their eyes met.

'I don't know!' Leaning on the gas fire, their hands pressed over their mouths, they began simultaneously to giggle.

'Suppose it's a rat?'

'Oh no,' said Annie, instantly sober. The sound stopped, as suddenly as it had begun. 'I don't think I – couldn't we get someone in, or something?'

'Who?'

'I don't know. Pest control. The council. I don't know.'

'The police? The fire brigade?'

'All right, all right. Where's the torch?' Annie still felt

160

slightly prone to giggle, excited, as if she had had just enough wine at a party. 'And don't mention the fire brigade, please.' She took hold of the gas fire, and went on chattily, 'Wasn't that weird, we thought it was you for a minute, having an uncontrollable blaze' – she pulled hard, harder, the thing was just shifting – 'up here all by yourself, they were very nice about it, it happens all the time apparently, oh—'Annie looked up, struck by a sudden thought, 'did you turn the gas off up here?'

'Yes. Can it come out any more?'

'Just a sec. There, try now.'

Squinting, Janet held the torch against the narrow crack between the gas fire and the wall, and lit the square black hole of the fireplace behind.

'Quick—'

In the darkness a flash, a twinned gleam, of eyes green-ish-gold in the torchlight.

'Got it?'

'Yes—' Small sharp beak, wings blurred with old soot.

'What is it?'

'It's okay, you can let go, it's a bird.'

'A bird. Oh. Funny. Must have fallen down the chimney then. Oh, poor thing. We'll have to get it out.'

'How?'

Annie turned round. Lewis was lying quite still on the rug, his eyes now and then closing. So that was all right.

'Unscrew these bits. Here, look. Just this one ought to do it.'

'Then what?' There was a pause, while both of them imagined the bird launching itself at their faces, hurling itself round the room with its bony claws splayed, perhaps uttering horrible cries, and spattering greasy soot, and crashing into something and hurting itself and dying wretchedly just when it should have been saved.

'It might jump at the light.'

'Yes,' said Janet. Funny, now that she knew it was only a bird, how easy it was to imagine herself there, fallen by

161

some accident into the airless darkness; she could just see the crack of light above her head as Annie had heaved at the gas fire, imagine the blinding painful glare of the torch in her own dazzled eyes.

'We should turn the light off,' she said, 'and open the window, then it'll look light outside and it can fly straight out.'

'Carry it to the window.'

'Yes. You hold the fire,' said Janet, 'and I'll pick it up. All right?'

'Right.' We're going to save you, thought Annie at the bird, you'll be all right now. She felt tremendously excited, barely able to keep still. We're going to save you!

'I've got a screwdriver,' said Janet, 'hang on.' In the kitchen she found that her hands were trembling a little. She picked her rubber gloves up, put them down again, no, too bulky, might make me drop it or hurt it somehow. Besides she wanted to touch the bird, she longed to feel its little light body in her gentle hand. She felt a sort of gratitude to it, for putting itself in a danger from which she could rescue it. After all those birds and animals you saw lying dead along the verge, she thought, and the badgers and rabbits and young foxes that must have stepped out so hesitantly, so unknowingly into the main road to meet death there, this time I can do something, this time I can stop the fox and turn it back to the field, no, not that way, this way—

She hurried back to the front room, half anxious that Annie might have got to work on her own, but Annie was leaning over the table fiddling with the window bolt.

'Jolly stiff this' she said, looking round and grinning. 'You'll have to get on to the landlady about it.'

'I mean,' said Marion, drawing her fork across the table-cloth so that it left a track of faint parallel lines, 'do you mind if I ask you some questions about it, because—'

'No—'

'Because I keep sort of thinking about it, I don't know what to—' She stopped, and took another gulp of wine. They were halfway through the bottle already.

'What I mean is—' She lowered her voice, glanced round, but the place was fairly empty, and not a waiter in sight, 'I must say I don't think much of the service,' she said, 'it's what, it's practically twenty minutes, it's not as if they're busy, is it, I just can't bear to think of you, you know, shafting one another,' she finished violently, and looked down at the tablecloth again.

Was that the real problem, she wondered. Well, it was one of them. The brutality of that act, wasn't that what they did in bed together, men?

'And I don't know which is worse,' she added, painfully grinning, 'him doing it to you or you doing it to him, I mean I just can't imagine it and I sort of keep trying to, I don't want to, I just—'

'Well, stop trying. We didn't do that. Actually.'

'Oh. Didn't you?'

'No. We did try. Once or twice. But we couldn't. We kept laughing.'

'Laughing?' Marion was startled. Laughing?

Benny was smiling across the table at her. 'It's not as easy', he said, 'as you might think.'

'Isn't it?'

'It was just – funny, we kept getting, you know, helpless, giggling. So we stopped.'

'Oh. So. What did you do, then, I mean, if you don't mind me asking, do you?'

'No. Well. We just, you know—'

'I don't know!' Almost laughing herself.

'Played with one another,' said Benny. He sounded mildly exasperated, the tone he used when she was being dense trying to map-read. 'Does it matter?'

'Yes. I don't know why.' Though that was not true, thought Marion. The image now was of them lying together laughing, an image of love anyone might understand. Or enjoy.

'And you've never . . . had an affair . . . with any other man?'

'No.'

'What about Mel?'

Benny shrugged.

'What, you don't know?'

'Of course I know, it's just not your business, is it? But yes, if you must know. Not now though. Not for ages, as far as I know.'

Marion sighed, and sat back, and a waiter appeared at her elbow, with two plates of tortellini.

'Thanks.'

'Enjoy your meal.'

'I always want to tell them to sod off, when they say that,' said Benny mildly, picking up his fork when the waiter had gone.

'Yes, it's sort of rude, isn't it, somehow,' said Marion. She felt cheerful, suddenly, and hopeful. 'He was more that way than you then,' she added.

Benny swallowed. 'Look. Just don't start thinking it was all him. He didn't seduce me or anything, he didn't bully me into it, he was only a couple of years older than I was. I loved him. I really loved him, and if that was what he wanted it was all right by me.'

'Suppose you'd said No, though. What then?'

'I didn't, did I? Well. If I'd said no we wouldn't have been friends any more. I mean, that was clear enough. And I didn't want that.'

'So it was more him, then.'

'I was eighteen! You don't know what it was like.'

'What was it like, tell me.'

'When you're eighteen. I was seeing Mel, and girls. I had two regular girlfriends as well at one point, I was sleeping with three different people all at once, it was – it was wonderful, it was so exciting, all those people desiring me, and there were always girls, there was always, like, a party.'

'Did he love you, d'you think?'

'Of course. But not as much as I loved him.'

'Do you still love him?'

'Yes.'

More than me?

'I won't hear a word against him,' said Benny. 'What would I have been without him? I would never have done anything without him, maybe it's all gone now but it was me that threw it all away. All the success I've had, it's all down to him, everything but you.'

'Me?'

'You were my chance. You and Lewis.'

'Oh, Benny—'

'I'm sorry it's all gone wrong. But I don't think I can do it, I don't seem to know how to do it, you know, families. Oh, don't cry, Marion, please—'

'You loved him more than me.'

'Oh, no, oh, look, look at me, Marion, it was never like us, honestly, I loved him but I used to get drunk, I mean, I used to have to get drunk, I used to pretend it wasn't happening to me—'

'But that's worse, it means you would do anything for love, anything,' said Marion, crying outright now.

'Who wouldn't?' said Benny.

Russell parked the motorbike beneath a lamp-post and nipped back to Miss Grey's house, passing it just to check and then carrying on to the end of the street while he thought out what to do. One light on, downstairs. Perhaps they were all in there. In which case there was nothing doing, bar a little broken glass, maybe, on the path, there were plenty of handy milk bottles around.

On the other hand lots of people went out leaving one light on. He pressed his elbow against the thin sheet of

165

steel in his pocket again. Ring the bell, risk it? He'd hear anyone coming to the door, after all, you nearly always did, there would be plenty of time to make off. He could just stick the crash helmet back on and run for it, be yet another in the small series of unusual or slightly threatening incidents which by now, he hoped, were beginning seriously to unnerve her.

The street was very quiet. Russell made his way cautiously down the path, trying to look casual, in case of curtain-twitchers. As he reached the door a sudden noise from above made him jump. He looked up fast, and what he saw made his backbone give a curious flicking shudder, like lightning top to bottom: from two storeys up, high above his head, something, some creature, a bird, shot squawking out of a window, went like a bullet across the street, and disappeared over the rooftops still uttering its strange, hoarse, tearing cry.

Russell instinctively ducked, and the hairs on his neck prickled upright. He stood for a moment, hesitating. For an instant he remembered with vivid clarity the feel of cold fur against his cheek, pressing against his face in gentle suffocation. He felt blank, as if he could only wait, as if, he was to tell himself later much later, he had known all the time that something terrible, demonic, was waiting there for him, lying coiled behind the door. His gloved hand reached out all the same. He watched it, the forefinger pointing, swinging slowly up to meet the bell. He pressed it. The something happened. The door seemed to rock, gently, on its hinges, to shudder in its frame; for a tiny part of a second it bulged towards him, as if pressed from behind by some gigantic force. Russell opened his mouth to scream, NO! and as he turned, something enormous, like a great hand, seemed to lift him up, lifted him violently off his feet and flung him backwards, rushing him through the air and hurling him with a terrible thud onto the unbelievable hardness of the concrete gatepost at the end of the path, where for a very long time, or a second or so,

166

he lay too stunned even to breathe, just lay there broken, while a roar of flame burst, twin dragons, through the broken door and the exploding shattering front-room window, lighting up shreds of curtains to coil and flutter as if alive in the light evening breeze.

Russell rolled over, crawled fast as clockwork out into the street, where already doors were opening and people running and shouting. Someone ran to him, pulling and calling, and Russell, aware of no pain, shouting now himself, begging them to let him go, please, please, sank suddenly into a burning and flashing darkness.

Marion and Benny decided to walk home. It was a beautiful evening, Marion said, the sort that makes you think spring can't be too far away. They held hands, stopping every now and then to kiss, 'I'm sorry, I can't keep my hands off you,' Marion laughed, breathlessly, and it was true, he was delectable, she opened his coat to touch his skin through his shirt.

'Am I weird?' she asked, as they stood beneath a lamppost, embracing. 'It's the thought of you, and him, it's sort of, ah—'

'Erotic?'

'Yes, is it funny?'

'Yup.'

'Well, I mean, men are supposed to find lesbians exciting, aren't they, they're always cropping up in porn magazines and so on. Aren't they?'

'Well, I think that's because, you know, you're meant to think about joining in.'

'Oh.' Marion considered this. For a moment she allowed herself to look properly at the images that had, ever since that weekend, tormented her. They were, by and large, she thought, undressing images, caressing preliminaries, fantasies not so much of sex outright as of romance. Would I

167

still feel like this, she wondered, if he and Mel had done all the things men can do?

She would have preferred the answer to be No, feeling vaguely that to be aroused by the idea of two beautiful young men caressing one another was on the whole less perverse than being aroused by the idea of them actually coming to grips; but it is Yes, she thought, no point trying to think otherwise.

She looked up, and kissed him again, and the inward shift and sinking of desire she felt made the breast-feeding pleasure seem like the merest cursory twitch.

'I wouldn't worry about it, if I were you,' said Benny. 'What's the point? No one understands sex, there's too much to know.'

'You don't, well, mind, then?' But of course he doesn't, she thought, as he laughed at her, nothing matters to him as much as being desired. No wonder Mel could do what he liked with him, fresh from his ghastly parents' hands as he must have been. And of course that is part of the eroticism, for me, she thought, it is that whiff of emotional coercion, knowing that it was not really what Benny wanted, that makes the caressing images all the more powerful. I don't know what that makes me. Best, perhaps, not to think about it too hard.

'Let's get home,' said Benny. 'Lewis'll be asleep.'

'So he will. Better be anyway.'

They walked on, still entwined. A couple of fire engines and an ambulance shot past them, sirens blaring, but that was nothing unusual. They took no notice.

Annie had had time to turn round from the window, to begin articulating the thought, Suppose it preens itself, and gets all that soot inside it, and still dies, perhaps we should have tried to wash it or something—

She had opened her mouth to start on this as the first

explosion rocked the floor, knocking her over sideways against the edge of the table.

'What?'

'Shut the window, shut the fucking window!'

'What?'

Annie struggled to her feet, Janet was kicking the door shut. 'Stairs are on fire!'

Lewis, Lewis, Annie spun round, but Janet had already grabbed him. 'The stairs are on fire,' said Janet again, 'put the rug at the door, no, roll it up, along the door, quick!'

Annie ran, blundering into Janet, her legs shaking, her hands numb. Behind the door she could hear an immense roaring. She felt very cold. She stuffed the rug along the door, and her voice said, 'Now what?'

Her voice was perfectly calm, ready for anything, and at the sound of it Annie herself drew back from panic, ready to trust her voice, as if it were the sound of her soul or something else eternal and unflappable.

'Now what?'

Janet's voice was also quite calm. 'We get him out.'

Annie ran back to the window.

'We'll have to open it.'

'I know. But if we wait a bit it'll give us a bit more time.'

'Wrap him up. What can we wrap him in?'

I am not here. I am saving Lewis. He is here. I am not. This is not happening to me.

'My jacket. On the door.'

He was awake now, and whimpering. 'There there,' said Janet absently, folding the leather round him, tying the sleeves across his little chest.

'Will they be there?'

'Now, do you think?'

They looked at one another. To open the window would fan the flames; the fire might kick down the door and hurl itself across the room.

'Now.'

Annie flung up the window and hung out of it. They

were in the street, dozens of upturned faces, mouths opening, she could hear nothing over the blazing voice of the fire, but there, yes, a blanket, something that could be a blanket, men running, waving their arms. She pulled her head back in.

'We'll have to throw him,' she said, 'we can't just drop him, we've got to throw him over the fire.'

'Where. Let me see.'

'Or we could wait, I don't know how long they will take.'

'I don't want to risk it, do you?'

'Shall I do it?'

'I will,' said Janet. I will save him. She turned back to the window, leant out with Lewis bundled in her arms, briefly measured the distance, and threw.

Peter, walking past the stationary traffic, turned a corner and began to smell smoke, noticed suddenly that the air was thick with it. The street was crowded, no more or less than usual, and no one – he listened as couples went by – seemed to be talking about any fire. But there were flakes now, of soot, landing on his hand and getting in his face, his eyes began to itch. He hurried on, coughing, there were more people about now, and excited little groups of them on corners.

'A bomb, wasn't it?'

'Heard it go off, I thought, what the hell's that, I ran out—'

In the middle of the road a policeman was halting traffic, leaning in to each driver's window, saying something; the cars were then laboriously turning round. The road was closed. Marion's road.

Peter hesitated, went over.

'Excuse me—' he began.

'Road's closed,' said the policeman. He was young, and hoarsely cockney. 'Whole block's on fire back there.'

'What!'

'Can't get past, sir. No-go.'

'But I'm going there, I know someone there, my sister-in-law—'

'Emergency vehicles all there sir, nothing you can do except stay out of their way, all right?'

For a miserable moment Peter hung about, not sure whether the policeman had actually forbidden him to walk past him, but resentfully unwilling to disobey him if he had; after a few seconds' worth of shuffling about arguing with himself it occurred to him that the policeman was all on his own with about a hundred cars a minute to deal with, that he wasn't even looking; Peter ran, head down, shoulders hunched, half-expecting to be rugby tackled from behind, but no one even seemed to notice him, and there was a crowd to blend in with as soon as he got round the corner, a crowd clearly, he saw straight away, rather enjoying itself, chatty as a party, milling about behind frail barriers of yellow sticky tape. Lights flashed, blue, scorching gold, real firemen were everywhere, costumed, with real hatchets hanging from their belts and those helmets, they still wore helmets like that, did they? and it was her house, it was really her house, and clearly some of the house next door. Peter took someone by the shoulder.

'What happened, please, I know her, her house, what happened?'

'You a relation?'

Oh God, the baby too.

'Yes.'

'You want to talk to him, bloke over there, see?'

Another fireman in his comic hat. Peter ducked beneath the plastic ribbon.

'Please, what happened, is anyone, she's my sister—'

Annie visiting. A Wednesday usually. What day was it now? Peter could not remember.

'Everything's under control now sir, you just take it easy—'

'Who was there, who was in there, are they all right?'

171

'You come with me, sir, I'll check which hospital—'
'Hospital—'
You found her, did you sir?
Yes. I found her.
'I've got the names here—'
Annie, it was Annie, the name jumped out at him.
'Ambulance left a good ten minutes ago, sir—'
'Annabel,' said Peter, and covered his eyes.

26

'THE FUNNY THING IS,' SIGHED ANNIE, 'HE WAS
probably in more danger from us than he was from the
fire.'

'How d'you work that out?'

'Well, chucking him out from the third floor. I mean
God Almighty. If someone had just dropped their edge of
blanket or something—'

'Well, they didn't, did they?'

'We should have waited.'

'Look,' said Peter, 'I think you're absolutely crackers
even thinking about it, I mean, he's all right, isn't he, it
was a crisis, you saved him, didn't you, it's mad saying you
saved him the wrong way. You weren't to know how quick
they'd be. I think you were marvellous. Personally.'

Annie shook her head, but she was smiling.

'We were just lucky.' She looked up: 'Hallo, Joe, how
are you?'

'Hallo, you. Have you got time for another, when does it
start?'

'Fifteen minutes. Yes please.'

Joe headed for the bar.

'Is, is Janet going to be in it?'

Annie nodded. 'She reckoned she'd be all right for most

of it, even if she had to mime the last bits. She's still a bit croaky.'

'Funny it's my dad's choir. His last performance though, did I tell you?'

'No. Why's that?'

'Oh, something about the conductor, dad made some sort of stand and the vote went against him, he thought the rest of the committee would back him up and they didn't. So he's had to resign.'

'Oh. Poor old Stanley. Is he upset?'

Peter shrugged. He had not, he realised, given the question much thought, what with one thing and another. He gave it some now. How long had the old boy been in the choir anyway? Had to be, what, at least thirty years. Every Tuesday night for thirty years, and in charge of nearly everything for close on ten. Concentrating, Peter replayed his quick drink with his father earlier that evening. 'Going to miss it,' Stanley had said, eyeing his half pint, but even so Peter could not hear anything other than mild resignation in these words. It did not occur to him that this might be assumed, for he had never counted himself amongst those his father might wish to deceive.

'It's a bit hard to tell,' he said at last. 'You can ask him at the interval if you like, he's coming up. He's really pleased. About you and me, I mean.'

'Is he? Good.' But why? wondered Annie. He doesn't like me that much. And my mother's never really gone for Peter either; what was she so happy about?

Peter noticed the frown. 'You'll stop thinking about it eventually. Just so long as you don't try too hard not to think about it at first.'

'It's that first bang, when it knocked me over, that's what keeps coming back. And this feeling, that it wasn't really happening, I've thought, is this how people do the most heroic things, you know, rescue other people and so on? It's this very strong sensation that it isn't really happening. I felt so calm, we just had this problem, which was how to

174

get Lewis out, nothing else. I keep getting that feeling back: this isn't hapening. D'you know what I mean? Oh, thanks, Joe.'

'What sort of bird was it, that's what I want to know,' said Joe lightly. 'Saved by a starling.'

'I don't know. It didn't half cluck flying off.'

'And what is it telling all the other starlings,' said Peter, but then had such a vivid mental picture of a lone rhinoceros that he fell silent, puzzling over it.

'What about the mystery man at the doorbell, did you find out any more about him?'

Annie shook her head. 'No. I can't seem to find the right person to ask. But if he hadn't been there—'

'You'd have smelt gas when you were coming downstairs,' said Peter. 'None of it would have happened.'

'I've thought about that,' said Annie eagerly, 'and I think it would; I mean, I know what I should have done now, God knows I've had enough people telling me what I should have done, but I didn't know then, d'you see?' She sighed. 'I'd have come down to the half landing. Smelt the gas, it must have been pouring out by then. I'm pretty sure that I'd have just done it automatically: put the light on.'

'Ah,' said Joe.

'Yes. I wouldn't have thought about it. I'd have thought, What's going on down there? And I'd've flicked the switch.'

'Holding Lewis,' said Peter, regretting it instantly as he saw Annie's face.

'Oh yes. Holding Lewis.'

'How is Marion, anyway?'

'She's all right. All things considered. She doesn't know whether to be grateful to me or not,' said Annie, half laughing, 'I mean it would be all right if we'd chucked the baby out and then got killed when the floor collapsed or something, as it is she doesn't quite know what to think. She's got back with Benny, though.'

'Yeah.' There was a pause. 'Well, I suppose she knows what she's doing.'

175

'I thought it might be the shock,' said Annie gloomily.

'We ought to be going, I think that was the last bell.'

They rose, collecting their coats, Joe gulping at his beer.

'Where's Janet staying now, she all right, d'you know?'

'Yes, some friend of hers, she said. Someone in the choir actually. Oh. Look, if she comes up in the interval, can you not say anything about how we should have waited, I think she still thinks we did the right thing, I sort of don't want her to—'

'Sure, sure,' said Peter. 'Anyway I still think you did too.'

'It was only the starling we saved.'

'It saved you. Killed by a cat and saved by a bird, it's quite poetic really.'

'What's this about a cat?' asked Joe, as they made their way to their seats. The orchestra was already in place, making pleasant tuning-up noises.

'Muff,' whispered Annie, as the choir began to file on stage. 'Look, there's Janet! And Stanley. Doesn't he look smart. Marion's cat. It kept peeing in the hallway, it was a real nuisance, she was always mopping up, it did it that night. Anyway all those months of cat pee—' she dropped her voice as the tuning stopped and the audience grew quiet '—must have dripped through the floorboards, the gas pipe was underneath you see, corroded, the last time it must've just broken through all of a sudden, while I was upstairs.'

The lead violinist climbed on stage, to polite applause.

'Place is packed,' said Peter, looking round.

And the conductor, with another fattish bald bloke in evening dress, a soloist, thought Joe, his heart sinking. Hours lay ahead, he thought, hours of being warbled or bawled at. What am I doing here? he wondered, as he had wondered so often, for years, when in Peter's company. A thought struck him.

'What happened to it?'

176

'Happened to what?' whispered Annie. The conductor raised his baton; the choir rose, like an army, to its feet. A silence fell.

'The cat,' whispered Joe, but Annie could only shake her head, for the concert had begun.

There, oh, there they are, thought Janet on the stage. It was the movement of Annie's hair that had caught her eye. Does she know I've seen her? Wish I could wave.

More scared than I was when the house was on fire. Shaking all over. Don't let me sing in the wrong place. Don't let me turn over two pages at once.

Oh, Lord—

A mile away the adverts were still on, but Russell was uncomfortable already, as there was a particular place deep inside the plaster that itched so persistently that he sometimes felt he could almost see the feather trapped there, or the breadcrumb. Using his other foot he pushed the plastered leg sideways out into the aisle, and tried clenching various parts of it, which hurt so much that he had to groan once or twice, so that Vicki leant forward with her caring face on.

'Are you all right?'

Shut up, thought Russell venomously. But I can't get home on my own, can I? Not yet, anyway.

'I'm okay,' he hissed back.

'Of course he was really attempting a palace revolution,' said Mrs Downely over her quick gin in the interval, 'and since he didn't have the ground support all he actually did was draw attention to the fact that things needed changing. And so we were swept with revolutionary fervour. I thought the tide turned remarkably quickly, don't you? As soon as that soprano stood up and said how much her French evening classes cost. Poor Stanley hadn't a leg to stand on after that.'

'But he – I thought he more or less ran the choir,' said Janet. Cautiously she eyed Stanley over the rim of her glass. He seemed cheerful enough, chatting to Annie over there.

'Well, he did, and of course he wasn't making a very good job of it lately, there is really too much for one person to do. He will leave rather a gap, but I'm sure there will be all sorts of power-hungry types ready to fill it, from the ranks. A new committee, purged of the old guard. A post-revolutionary atmosphere of wild creative endeavour. An underground pro-Stanley movement, grumbling in pubs, reminiscing about the old days, wondering where they went wrong. Accusations of counter-revolution, fresh purges; really choirs are just like gardening, they positively bristle with metaphors for society at large. Hallo, Stanley, I was just talking about you. It's going very well, isn't it?'

'Absolutely full house,' said Stanley. 'Hallo,' he said shyly to Janet. 'I hope you're fully recovered?'

'Yes. Thank you.'

'I'm very sorry you'll be leaving us,' said Mrs Downely.

'Going to miss it,' said Stanley lightly. 'Break a leg, now.' He moved off.

'Oh dear,' said Mrs Downely, watching him briefly join another chattering circle. 'He always does this at a concert, you know, rallying the troops or something. And now for the last time. They are getting up a collection for him, isn't it awful! The choral equivalent of being forced into exile I suppose, or machined-gunned in a cellar. Actually if I were Stanley I think I might prefer the firing squad to accepting a cut-glass bowl and a pile of coffee table books from the very people who'd thrown me out in the first place, wouldn't you? I'm glad he's leaving. Shows a proper spirit. Better than the rest of the old committee, all grousing away on the back benches. At least he has done the honourable thing.'

'What was that about breaking legs?' asked Janet.

'Her aunt, or something,' Annie was saying. Joe looked across without interest. A whole hour more, he thought. If only you could bring a book to read, the trouble with just sitting there was that you had to think all the time, there was nothing to stop you day-dreaming about all sorts of things best left undisturbed. I listened properly to what, a couple of minutes? When the orchestra first started, becaused they sounded so real, and then when they all started singing . . . the conductor waving his arms, struggling on his podium like someone trying to dance with his shoes nailed down, that bass soloist, looked as though his suit would burst . . . wish it had . . . Joe yawned violently.

A bell rang. Annie jumped.

'About this cat,' said Joe suddenly, 'what happened to the cat?'

'Time we were off,' said Mrs Downely.

'I've thought,' said Janet as they trooped back to the green room to assemble for the second half, 'about what you said.'

'About writing to him?'

Janet nodded. 'I think it might work.'

'Make you feel better?'

'Yes.'

'Do it straight away then. Then, when he decides he wants to find you – and of course you have to be prepared for him not to want to, there's no guarantee, is there? But if he tries to find you make sure there's a whole sheaf of letters. The more the better, the further back the better, do you see? The more years you have regretted it the better, as far as he's concerned.'

'Yes.'

'It's not much. But it is an active step. And it will help to make you real for him, I mean, less like someone he has somehow made up on the spot. It will help to give you a past.' But she will have to be careful, waiting for him, thought Mrs Downely. Absence of personal fear is all very well at my age, but it is hardly right at hers. Perhaps that is what I recognised, when I first saw her. 'Hope you've got enough puff for *Belshazzar*,' she added.

'Oh,' said Janet, 'you didn't mention anything about the fire to Annie, did you, I think she still thinks we did the right thing—'

'Hardly spoke to her. Anyway you've forgotten the smoke. If it made you feel rather ill for a while, what would it have done to a baby?'

'Well, possibly less harm than being thrown out of a third floor window.'

'Have it your own way. Oh, I do love *Belshazzar*. I shan't sleep a wink tonight. The music gets in my head and goes round and round. Still at least it will drive out the remnants of my pathetic mugger. And it will be worth it anyway. I even suspect the audience will enjoy some of it, poor things.'

'In the back garden all the time.'
    'Oh.'

'I can't stand this,' said Russell, 'I'm getting out.'
    'Shall I come with you?'
    'No, I'll be okay, I'll just wait outside, it's nearly over—'
    'No, I don't care, I'll come too—'
Pursued by flames and explosions they made their halting way up the aisle to the foyer and sudden quiet. The kiosk was closed, one or two ushers stood aimlessly waiting for the stampede at the end.

'Sorry,' said Russell. His heart was still pounding.

'I should have realised. I should have thought. It was bound to be a bit much, after all you've been through. We should have gone to see something, you know, a bit calmer. A comedy or something.'

'Mary Poppins'd be a bit much at the moment actually,' said Russell. Eight quid down the drain though. 'You should have stayed, now we won't know how it ended.'

'I'd rather be with you,' said Vicki, squeezing his arm.

The air was fresh and cold outside. At the bus stop Vicki suddenly pointed.

'Oh, look!'

'What?'

'Can you hear it? There, up there, look!'

Russell looked up, and at once began to hear birdsong.

'It's a blackbird, listen!'

He saw its little swelling throat, profiled in shadow on some Gothic piece of ironmongery high above the square.

'What's it think it's doing? They're not supposed to be nocturnal. Are they?'

'I don't think so. Perhaps the lights have confused it. Isn't it lovely, Russell?'

Odd. There it was, singing away in Leicester Square, and you could almost hear a sort of rural quiet round it, as if the quiet were carried in the song. Then again, maybe it was like the pigeons that lived in railway stations, and had horrible things wrong with their feet, decultured, degraded, the birdlife equivalent of all those human tribes done over by the First World, Aztecs and Amazonian Indians and whatnot. Perhaps the song was all wrong, and only another blackbird would be able to tell.

'I didn't know they'd moved into cities, did you, Russell?'

A new variant perhaps, an umpteenth generation immigrant completely at home, perhaps there were hordes of them all over the city.

At this something clicked in Russell's mind, and he took a sudden breath, for he had nearly remembered the terrible

181

bird of omen that had shot crying over his head before the door exploded and the great hand flung him to the ground.

'Russell?'

'I—'

'You all right?'

'Just – Yeah. I thought I'd remembered something for a minute.'

'What?'

Russell shook his head. 'Gone again.' He became aware, again, of the blackbird's song. *What was I thinking about?* Vaguely his memory showed him an ancient schoolroom map full of pointing arrows and little ships bristling with oars: the Dark Ages. Here the Jutes, there the Saxons. Who though could chart the history of animals and birds, empires rising and falling, invasions, massacres, uneasy settlements, integrations? *All those separate worlds*, thought Russell, *all those separate worlds that hardly touch. Here the Jutes, there the Saxons, there for all we know the songthrush, there the bank vole—*

'What's so funny?'

'Nothing,' said Russell, meekly. 'I was just listening.'

Above their heads the birdsong rose and fell.

Coda

ALL THIS HAPPENED A GOOD FEW YEARS AGO NOW. Peter and Annie married and bought a house together, and had a baby girl three years later: Rebecca, Stanley's dearest darling. By the time Annie was ready to go back to work her job had unfortunately disappeared, due to the latest round of health service changes; the legal ramifications of this are so complicated that she is still waiting for her case to be brought before the right industrial tribunal.

Peter has been promoted again, so they are not too badly off, but he has very little free time. Most of his thesis is still in the boxes the removal men supplied, and one of these, in a corner of the attic, has been home for a whole winter now to a growing family of mice, which have made themselves very comfortable on the soft shredded paper.

Marion and Benny split up for good soon after their reconciliation. Lewis has grown rather tall for his age, and Marion often has trouble getting him out of bed in time for school. Benny does not see his son very often. Mel has not asked him to join in any more tours, and he is currently working as a chauffeur, and going out with a woman he met at Alcoholics Anonymous.

Joe has become rather distinguished, in his own small field. He attends a great many conferences abroad. He takes Annabel with him, smiling from her pool in the Howgills. Sometimes he wonders if he should not find himself another therapist, or go back to the old one, but so far has decided on balance that he would rather not go through all that again. Some things are just irrevocable, he tells himself, and that's all there is to it. Supporting cast, that's me. And I'm all right anyway, look at old Pete now, never goes out any more, can't talk about anything but babies, who wants it? Howling and nappies and chicken-pox. I'm all right as I am.

Mel and Sophie had to have three attempts at IVF treatment. The twins were born two months prematurely, and spent weeks in intensive care, but survived. Sophie's hair has gone quite grey.

Vicki left Russell when he hit her twice in one week. For a while he was just able to make the mortgage payments on his own, but now he has a succession of more or less friendly lodgers to help him. The value of his flat has dropped by twenty thousand pounds. He is still working in the same hospital. He has rather a bad limp, and cannot run fast at all. Birds cry in his nightmares, but these are not very frequent.

Mrs Downely died in 1988. She had rather lost touch with Janet, who was thus all the more surprised to be left the grand flat in Mrs Downely's will. She lives there still. There are no more State Enrolled Nurses: a vast upgrading occurred, and Janet is currently a ward sister, though her hospital has recently been scheduled for closure. Perhaps her son has read her letter by now. She might hear from him any time, she thinks. She keeps herself busy while she waits. The flat is very tidy. She is still a member of the choir.